"Does it make you nervous that we're here alone?"

Actually the knowledge electrified her. She was being drawn to the flame, and to make matters worse she was enjoying it. "Should it?"

He dropped down beside her, so close his thigh was touching hers. As he slid his arm along the back of the couch, his eyes gleamed. He slowly smiled and she couldn't begin to guess what he was thinking. This man was supposed to be her prey, and instead he was preying on her, heating her insides, scrambling her thoughts.

"I would like to think that that makes you at least a little nervous." His deep, dark voice lit sparks along her nerves. "In fact, it'd be very good for my ego if that were the case."

A slight smile curved her lips as she shook her head. "The vast majority of the women at the party tonight were salivating over you, Jonah. You don't need me to stroke your ego."

His gaze dropped to her lips. "Maybe not my ego, but feel free to stroke any other part of me you'd like."

WHAT ARE *LOVESWEPT* ROMANCES?

They are stories of true romance and touching emotion. We believe those two very important ingredients are constants in our highly sensual and very believable stories in the LOVESWEPT line. Our goal is to give you, the reader, stories of consistently high quality that may sometimes make you laugh, sometimes make you cry, but are always fresh and creative and contain many delightful surprises within their pages.

Most romance fans read an enormous number of books. Those they truly love, they keep. Others may be traded with friends and soon forgotten. We hope that each LOVE-SWEPT romance will be a treasure—a "keeper." We will always try to publish

LOVE STORIES YOU'LL NEVER FORGET BY AUTHORS YOU'LL ALWAYS REMEMBER

The Editors

Loveswept ® 778

The Damaron Mark:

THE WARRIOR

FAYRENE PRESTON

BANTAM BOOKS

NEW YORK · TORONTO · LONDON · SYDNEY · AUCKLAND

THE DAMARON MARK: THE WARRIOR
A Bantam Book / March 1996

ISBN 0-553-44418-2

Published simultaneously in the United States and Canada

*Bantam Books are published by Bantam Books, a division of Bantam Dou-
bleday Dell Publishing Group, Inc. Its trademark, consisting of the words
"Bantam Books" and the portrayal of a rooster, is Registered in U.S.
Patent and Trademark Office and in other countries. Marca Registrada.
Bantam Books, 1540 Broadway, New York, New York 10036.*

ONE

The shrill sound of the security alarm knifed through the still night. Jolie froze. The din hurt her ears and turned her blood to ice. For one second fear paralyzed her.

Then her adrenaline slammed into overdrive. She bolted out of the back-terrace doors just as the rear lawn of the estate flooded with light.

Clad in black from head to toe, she ran from shadow to shadow. Black cloth shrouded the painting she had just stolen and that was now strapped to her back. Her heart was pounding hard, her breath was coming in gasps. The night air was warm, but her skin felt clammy.

She kept running—she had no choice. She had mere minutes before the police and security guards converged on the estate.

She stumbled and went down on one knee. The painting on her back shifted. She straightened it and took off running again.

The ten-foot wall that marked the edge of the back lawn loomed ahead of her, her last obstacle. Shadowed by the branches of an oak tree, her rope ladder hung over the wall, waiting.

In the distance she heard the wail of police sirens. She lunged at the rope, but missed the bottom rung. She lost her balance, her footing. She could barely see; her eyes were stinging and watering badly. She rubbed them, trying to clear her vision.

The sirens were louder now, closer. Once again she grabbed for the rope, but her hands slipped along its length and its coarse fibers burned the tender skin of her palms. She cried out with pain before she could stop herself.

After a moment she managed to regain her grip and footing and she scrambled up the ladder and over the wall to the ground on the other side. Sharp needles of pain shot up her legs as she landed.

The sirens sounded as if they were at the house now. The police and security would come in the front, but within minutes of their arrival they would circle around to the back.

Her time had just run out.

She pulled the ladder down after her, but didn't bother to gather it up properly. She took off running toward her car with the ladder dragging along the ground behind her. She was wheezing badly, each breath a struggle, each breath a fiery stab.

The ladder snagged on a branch; she was jerked backward. Precious seconds ticked by while she untangled it.

She was never going to make it. They were going to catch her this time. She began to run, to pray.

Finally she reached the car, but she dropped the keys once, twice. At last she managed to open the trunk. She threw the ladder in, then more carefully placed the painting on top of the rope. In the car, she drove as fast as she dared down the New York country back road, her lights out.

The quarter moon was of minimal help, showing the landscape as shades of black and dark gray. Before tonight she had done her best to memorize the road, but still she was basically driving blind. God, she was scared.

Focus, she ordered herself. Focus.

She had a choice to make. If she continued down the road she was on, she would risk meeting the police. If she cut across a field, she'd have a better chance of eluding them. However, she'd have to find the break in the fence that had occurred in the last four days. To find it she'd have to slow down. Besides, her four-door sedan didn't do its best off-road, the sedan she drove because a four-wheel-drive vehicle would draw too much attention.

She swiped her hand over her eyes, attempting to clear her vision. She'd been wrong. She had no choice.

She jammed the accelerator to the floor and raced down the road until she came to the first crossroad. To her left, the lights of a police car were approaching fast. She slid her car around the corner and headed in the opposite direction. By the time the police cars turned onto the road she had just been on, she was far enough away that they couldn't see her.

Still she didn't relax. She drove another mile, making sure the police were not on her tail, before switching on her headlights. Only then did she reach into her pocket for her prescription inhaler.

Quietly she opened the back door of the house she'd lived in her whole life. Passing through the small hall, she made her way into the kitchen. Even though she knew her father would probably still be awake, her heart sank as she saw him, sitting at the kitchen table. As much as she loved him, she wasn't up to conversation.

"I was hoping you'd be asleep, Papa. It's almost three A.M."

She always wrapped a bright red cape

around her all-black outfit upon her arrival home in case she encountered him, but the truth was, he never noticed what she wore. He didn't this time either.

He glanced up from the paper he'd been reading, a smile of greeting on his tired, lined face. "It is? I'm afraid I don't sleep much anymore, a bothersome trait it seems my daughter shares with me. Where have you been?" he asked, as an afterthought.

As exhausted as the episode at the Vandergriffs' estate had left her, she was still so wound up it would be hours before she would be able to sleep. "Out with Miranda and the gang."

She went straight to the cabinet where she kept her allergy medication and downed a couple of the pills, then dropped into a chair across from him. Miranda was a good friend of hers from college and she used the name shamelessly for occasions like this, along with a made-up gang of friends. In fact, her social life was nonexistent, much to Miranda's dismay. Fortunately her father was so wrapped up in his own private world, he rarely questioned her about specifics.

"That's nice." He took in her red eyes and nose. "Did one of them have a dog?"

"Two," she said, thinking of the guard dogs she had left tranquilized back at the estate. By now the security men would have seen that they were taken care of. Not that the tranquilizers would harm the dogs. When she'd first started out on her career of crime, she'd gone to great lengths to make sure of that.

"Have you taken your antihistamines?"

"Yes, just a minute ago." She didn't like to take them when she was on a job. In fact she didn't like to take them at any time. She never knew whether they would make her sleepy or revved up. The inhaler had managed to ease her chest tightness, but as always had left her with the shakes.

He gave an idle nod. "Good."

She smiled at him, reflecting how dear he was to her. Her mother had been able to keep him anchored in the real world when she'd been alive. They'd been happy then.

When she'd been small, he had spent hours with her at the seashore, helping her find pretty shells, building wondrous sand castles with her, enthralling her. But the nighttime had been her favorite time with her father. She'd crawl up on his lap and listen wide-eyed to the stories he told her of fairy princesses, their sleek, white unicorns, and their cuddly pet dragons that could toast marshmallows and heat cups of hot chocolate just by opening their mouths and blowing. When she grew older, he stopped telling her stories and instead would spend hours listening to her, to what was on her mind, to what was important to her.

But then six years ago her mother had died and everything had changed. Her father had retreated into his own world. Now his shaggy white hair rarely saw a comb or a pair of scissors unless she reminded him. And even though his work as an art professor and then as an art restorer had brought in excellent money over the years, he wore clothes even after they had become threadbare. His glasses were spotted with dust and flecks of paint.

He was absentminded about everything but his work, yet every once in a while he would surprise her with an astute observation. Like now.

"Your eyes look like a road map, Jolie Christiane. You need to rest and maybe eat something." And with that he returned his attention to his newspaper.

Accurate diagnosis, she reflected. Her nose was running, her eyes were stinging, and no doubt her face was dotted with bright red splotches. And on top of it all, her palms were throbbing with deep rope burns. She would need to wash them and treat them with antibiotic cream.

With a weary sigh she pushed herself up from the table and snagged a piece of hard candy for her shakes, then returned to the table. "What's so interesting in the paper?"

A sparkle appeared in his faded blue eyes. "The society pages, my dear. Jonah Damaron is holding a private showing in his home for his collection before he sends it out on tour."

"When?"

"Next week. And of course, as the artist who cleaned and restored three of his most important works, I'm cordially invited, along with a guest. Would you like to go?"

She couldn't think of anything she'd like less. She sighed again, only this time inwardly. "Of course."

"Good." He chuckled with glee. "You'll get to hear your old papa's work praised to the skies."

"I don't have to hear other people praise you to know that you're wonderful. I've told you before—I love you no matter what."

He nodded, but his attention had gone back to the newspaper and she had the feeling he hadn't even heard her. "You know," he said thoughtfully, "I haven't met Jonah Damaron yet. I'll be very eager to hear what he has to say about the work I've done for him."

"I thought he hired you."

"One of his assistants did."

"But you've been working for him for months. You mean he hasn't been in touch with you once?"

"He's been out of the country, but his assistant told me that Damaron had approved of my credentials."

"Is he still out of town?" she asked casually. She had to start finding out what she could about the man's schedule as soon as possible.

"Oh, I'm sure he's back by now. His party is less than a week away."

"He's got one or more assistants to plan parties, Papa."

"Uh-hum, well, I don't know."

Wealth brought layers, she had discovered. Layers of people who worked for the wealthy, buffering them and protecting them from other people and the more mundane details of life. And the more layers, the more complications for her. Before she broke into their homes, she had to make sure she knew where and what all the layers were.

"Look, here's his picture." He pointed to the paper. "He's a Damaron all right. Even in black-and-white, you can see that silver streak in his hair." He shoved the paper across the table to her.

Her first look at Jonah Damaron brought instant unease.

She was tired, that was all, she told herself. And her allergies had wrecked her system. She popped another piece of hard candy into her mouth and studied the photograph more carefully. Jonah Damaron's dark hair appeared jet-black, with the exception of the silver slash that ran straight back from his hairline above his right eyebrow. His eyes were light brown and they blazed off the page with their intensity.

There was a fair-haired beauty by his side. Her hand was curled around his arm and it looked as if she'd pulled him around just in time to have his picture taken so that he'd been caught in a candid moment. Even so, she would bet no one caught him completely unaware.

There was a dangerous glint of displeasure in his eyes, as if at the audacity of the unknown photographer who dared to take his picture. But there was also something else, a touch of humor, as if he saw the absurdity of the situation. In its own way, his humor was as dangerous as his displeasure. Both were knife sharp. And it was quite obvious to her that the picture would never have gone into the paper unless he had given his tacit approval.

There was a force about Jonah Damaron. It was there in his eyes, in his strong-boned features. Her unease grew. She found him threatening, somehow.

Strange that a photograph could affect her so.

She pushed the paper away. "I'm tired. I'm going to bed." She stood and dropped a kiss on her father's head. "And I would suggest that you do the same."

"Yes, yes, I will. Soon. See you in the morning."

Later she lay in bed, worrying about how tonight she'd slipped up, lost her concentration and made a serious mistake. Years ago she'd set out to make herself an expert on all kinds of alarms and security devices and she'd succeeded. But tonight she'd missed that last alarm.

Unacceptable.

It shouldn't have happened, but the fact that it had underscored what she'd been aware of for some time now. She'd been doing this too long.

She sighed. It didn't matter. Somehow she had to get her edge back, her sharpness, her skills. Because next week it was going to start all over again.

TWO

The room itself was a work of art, Jolie observed, standing apart from the milling black-tie crowd. Glittering chandeliers, dripping thousands of crystal droplets and beads, illuminated the throng of elegantly clad men and women. The colors they wore shimmered, the fine fabrics shifted and flowed, the gems glistened. But the focal point of the party was the extraordinary collection of French masters that hung along the length of the salon, each painting with its own specially designed lighting.

Waitresses and waiters glided up and down the salon dressed as the figures in the paintings. A dancer, wearing a full red skirt, looked ready to dance at the Moulin Rouge, or to be painted by Toulouse-Lautrec. A young woman dressed in Moroccan garb, complete with turban, could have stepped straight out of a Matisse painting. Several of Picasso's itinerant fairground entertainers were represented, from a Harlequin to an acrobat. A dour Cézanne woman in a tailored blue suit wore an eccentric hat adorned with green foliage, and served canapes.

And then there was Jonah Damaron.

She didn't know why her gaze kept going to him, not really. She told herself it was because she needed to keep track of him to make it easier to avoid him. But she wasn't sure she believed herself.

At the moment he was standing with several other Damarons. Easy to spot, the Damarons, even without the silver streak in their hair, which they all had. It was something about the way they moved and stood, claiming the space and the air and the energy around them, that identified them as members of their own exclusive clan. And they flowed toward one another, as if they all had the same internal compass that led them to other Damarons no matter who else was in the room.

But Jonah—to her mind, he stood out from the others. Even at the distance of the length of the salon, he had an absolutely riveting presence, as if he were an event of nature. His hair was a dark brown, it turned out, though in a certain light it came close to black. She couldn't tell what color his eyes were.

She watched as various women tried to

catch his attention, one after the other. In every case he responded with a polite, vaguely appreciative nod. But it was clear he was absorbed in conversation with the coolly magnetic man standing beside him who also had a single silver streak running through his raven hair. And no woman seemed able to pull his attention away.

Who was she? Jonah wondered, listening with half an ear as his cousin Sin made idle conversation beside him. There was nothing obvious about her. One had to look twice to detect the beauty that she really was. He had, and now he wasn't able to look away. Everything about her was quiet and understated, even the long black sheath she wore. Who was she?

He was puzzled. Even taking her beauty into account, he wasn't entirely sure why she had caught his attention.

Except . . . he knew the vast majority of the guests, and if he didn't know them personally, he knew the person with whom they had come. But the woman was a stranger. And though she didn't seem to be particularly interested in the art or the guests, she was definitely taking everything in. So what, he wondered, *was* she interested in?

Suddenly his arms were filled with an elegantly beautiful blonde. "Whoa." He laughed as he took his pregnant cousin's weight against him. "Be careful, Jo! You'll hurt yourself."

"Not a chance. I'm healthy as a horse." Smiling up at him, Joanna Damaron Whitfield playfully hit his arm. "But then how would you know? You've been gone too long. Lucky for you, you've come home when you have." She drew back and rubbed her round stomach. "Only two more months to go and you're going to have a new cousin."

He held up a hand, shielding his eyes. "Someone get me my sunglasses. You're glowing so much I bet Cale can find you in the dark."

She laughed. "Thank you for the compliment, but basically I've passed glowing and gone straight to fat."

Her husband came up behind her and put his hands on her shoulders. "I keep telling you, Jo—you're not fat. It's all baby."

She turned to him, her eyes wide with disbelief and happiness. "Cale, I *waddle*."

Sin grinned. "But you waddle with absolute grace, Jo."

She laughed again. "Family loyalty, there's nothing like it."

"I wouldn't lie to you." The glint in Sin's jade eyes told her that on this one subject he just might. "By the way, Lily can't wait to have a new cousin. She informed me the other night that she's tired of being the only one of her generation. She said she wanted cousins of her very own."

Jo's mouth dropped open. "She's four years old and she said *that*?"

Jonah spoke up. "Of course she said that. She's a brilliant child."

"Not that he's biased or anything," Sin said with a pleased smile. "Once she heard Jonah was back home, she wouldn't go to sleep until he came over to play with her."

Jonah shrugged. "What can I say? I'm irresistible to women."

Jo poked him in the chest. "I've noticed that about you."

"I was kidding."

She chuckled. "I wasn't."

"Lily's the one who's irresistible." He shook his head, his expression showing his amazement. "I can't believe how much she's grown since I last saw her."

"Kids have a way of doing that," Sin said.

Cale glanced around the room. "Speaking of irresistible women—where's Abigail?"

Sin's gaze searched for his great-aunt. "I saw her a minute ago, flirting outrageously and dazzling some poor besotted man who made the mistake of thinking he could conquer Abigail Damaron."

Jonah's glance returned to the woman who continued to intrigue him. She hadn't moved.

He had to fight not to suck in his breath at the sight of her. Lord, she *was* beautiful, but it wasn't only that which kept his gaze going back to her. No, there was something about her that struck a chord in him, he realized, and he wished he knew why. "Where's Kylie?" he asked, looking back at Jo, the question referring to her younger sister.

"She's still at school. She's got an exam first thing in the morning, then she'll be picked up and flown into the city for the family board meeting."

"Good. It'll be great to see her. It's hard for me to believe she's going to be a junior next year."

"She's had two great years in college. I'm very proud of her."

"We all are."

"Oh, look, Cale. Charlotte and Charles Kingsley just came in. I suppose we should make an effort to circulate. Let's go say hello." With a smile to her cousins, Jo took her husband's hand. "See you all later."

Cale threw a laugh over his shoulder at the two men. "She thinks I'll follow her anywhere. I wonder why."

After a moment Jonah heard Sin speak quietly. "Who is she?"

Jonah turned to his cousin. "Who's who?"

"The woman you keep looking at."

His mouth twisted into a wry grin. Sin

rarely missed a thing. "Have I been *that* obvious?"

"Only to me. So who is she?"

"I don't have a clue."

Sin's laugh was low and amused. "A situation I'm sure won't last long."

"Probably not."

Sin's expression slowly sobered. "What's wrong, Jonah? Something's bothering you—I can tell. Is it Hong Kong?"

"No. I told you—it's just about over. I'll give my full report tomorrow at the board meeting."

"And we can't wait." He paused. "We all know what you went through to accomplish what you did."

"Yeah," he said softly, his gaze resting on the mysterious woman. "But now I've come back."

"Coming back isn't always that easy, Jonah. Sometimes it takes time."

"Maybe." He shrugged. "I guess I'm a little tired." He thought for a moment. "No, that's wrong. I'm a *lot* tired." His smile flashed, then disappeared.

"We've been worried."

Jonah sliced him a glance. "Did you expect me to quit?"

"No, but there were times I wished you had. It was a damned near impossible job."

"But I could do it, and I did it. And at one

time or another I had help from nearly every member of the family."

"To some extent, that's true. But we didn't have to crawl through the sewers like you did."

"To catch scum you have to become scum," Jonah murmured, remembering the times he played outside the law and even sometimes reason. But then, he'd never been one to stay inside the lines. Too tidy. Too boring. "It took much too long," he said after a moment. "But I couldn't rest until it was done."

"So now you can."

"Can what?" His gaze had drifted back to the woman, and he wondered how one of the great masters would have interpreted her. Or even if they could have. They certainly wouldn't have been able to stay within the lines. There was something that seemed incredibly elusive about her.

"Now you can rest."

The laugh he gave held little humor. "I'm not sure I know how to rest. And you know what else?"

"What's that?"

Jonah looked at him. "I'm not sure I know how to relax with someone who is not family. Or if I know how to be with someone who does not come with complications."

"Take a long break, Jonah. Please."

He smiled faintly. "We'll see. Right now I'm not sure what I'm going to be doing for the next few months. But I *am* fairly positive what I'll be doing the rest of the evening."

Her father had positioned himself by the paintings he had restored, Jolie noted, basking in the oohs and ahs of admiration as people studied the art. He looked so happy. Since her mother's death he had come to live for his art and the acknowledgment and praise that came with it.

"Champagne?"

She shook her head at the young waitress dressed as a Degas dancer. From what she'd been able to ascertain so far, Jonah Damaron's security system was first-rate. But if she didn't find a way around it, she'd find a way through it. She always did. And she had a month. She just wished she didn't feel so on edge tonight, as if any way she turned she might step on a mine.

"Champagne?"

She was shaking her head even as she turned toward the waiter, but instead of one of the servers dressed as a nineteenth-century gentleman, she found Jonah Damaron, holding out a crystal flute to her. The *one* man in the entire room she did not want to talk to.

"No, thank you," she said, recovering with as much grace as she could. After all, the man was the host of the party. She couldn't very well snub him.

"Perhaps something else?"

"No, nothing." He was tall, big, leanly muscled. In another time his body would have served a warrior well. Now that he was nearby, she could see his eyes were golden brown, with fascinating glints of black. And at the moment they held traces of laughter.

She wondered what he found humorous.

She wondered at the dark shadows beneath his eyes.

She wondered why he had sought her out.

And most of all, she wondered how she would manage to handle the encounter.

Up close, the force she had merely sensed in him before was very real and quite enormous. Like everything else about him, the force was controlled. But she had the uneasy feeling that the control could slip away at any moment, leaving bare something extremely dangerous and barely civilized. Fortunately for her, she reflected wryly, this would only be a chance encounter. He was a host, circulating among his guests. Soon he would move on. Soon her heart rate would return to normal.

He sipped the champagne she had refused. "All right, then if I can't do anything for you, maybe you could do something for me."

"I can't imagine what that might be." She

schooled her nerves not to show. She could handle harmless banter, she told herself.

Jonah still didn't know what it was about her that struck the familiar chord in him, but he was very glad he was standing beside her. Her hair was a luxurious honey brown that fell a fingertip's length past her shoulders with an enticing suggestion of a curl. Her eyes were a soft doe brown that held a quiet intelligence and a subtle wariness. Her skin was the color of cream and gleamed with the texture of satin. At the moment he couldn't think of anyone who interested him more. "You could start with telling me your name."

"Ah good—an easy one." Harmless banter, she reminded herself. She needed to react to him as if he were any man and at the same time ignore the terrific pull of sensuality she felt from him, a sensuality she hadn't expected. She extended her hand to his. "I'm Jolie Lanier."

He enclosed her hand with his. "I'm Jonah Damaron."

She smiled because he had told her his name as if she wouldn't know. "I never doubted it."

"Excuse me?"

"I never doubted you were Jonah Damaron." Her smile broadened, and since he didn't seem inclined to release her hand, she tugged it free. "I saw your picture in the paper." She paused. "I gather it was an old picture."

"I don't know. I didn't see it. Why?"

She pointed to his eyes. "Those dark circles weren't in the picture."

"There's only one other person tonight who has mentioned the circles beneath my eyes and she was four years old."

"So I'm either rude or ingenuous." She grimaced. "Probably a bit of both." And both were completely uncharacteristic of her. "The truth is I don't know you, so those circles could be hereditary. I shouldn't have said anything. I apologize."

"No apology necessary, and they're not hereditary."

Somewhere along the line she'd made a mistake. She'd meant to brush him off, not draw more of his attention.

"The shadows come when I don't get enough sleep. And from other things."

If anyone in the world should be able to sleep, it should be Jonah Damaron, she thought. He had everything, didn't he? What were the demons that kept him awake? And why should she even be curious?

"What about you?" he asked.

Her lips twisted. "No dark circles."

"No, but could I have seen your picture in the paper?"

"Most unlikely." She purposefully didn't

elaborate, but as far as she knew, her picture had never been in any paper. She wouldn't allow it and it was an easy enough matter to control. She glanced at her father and wondered when he'd be ready to leave. And *surely* it was time for Jonah Damaron to move on to his next guest.

She wasn't entirely comfortable with the fact that he'd singled her out, Jonah sensed, studying her. Interesting. He couldn't think of one other woman in the room who *wouldn't* want his attention. The knowledge came not from conceit but from a fact that had been established early in his life. He glanced across the room at the man standing by a Renoir. "Any relation to Colbert Lanier?"

"My father."

"Your father's very talented."

She smiled. "You have no idea."

"Don't I?" It wasn't the first smile she had given him, but as before, it took him unaware. There was self-assurance in the smile, a certain confidence that told him no matter how much she might wish his attention elsewhere, she would not back down from him, not far at any rate. His gaze went to her full, sensual lips, covered with a shimmering sheen of gloss. He could remove it with one kiss. "Tell me," he said softly.

Her smile disappeared. "No—I'm sorry. Of course you have an idea. You hired him, right?" She'd been fooling herself. Nothing could be harmless with him, not even banter. Jonah Damaron wasn't just any man. He was a man she would be stealing from within the month. "Excuse me. I think I'll get a soda."

Subtle pressure on her arm stopped her. "Someone will bring it to you." He glanced around, caught the eye of a pretty Degas girl in a pink tutu. "May I have a soda, please?"

"Yes, sir," she said, and hurried off.

Jolie gazed after the girl. It was easier than looking at Jonah Damaron. The full power of his formidable intensity was focused on her, searing her skin, jangling her nerves. "Clever idea to have the servers dressed as the paintings."

"Isn't it?" He handed his champagne glass to another server and reached for her left hand. Lightly he stroked his finger over the third finger. "There's no indentation where a ring might have been recently."

His tone of voice indicated he had made a statement, yet she knew it was a question. "I don't wear jewelry."

"Not even a wedding ring?"

"Since I'm not married, no."

It was the information he was after, but it wasn't enough for him to release her hand. He liked the feel of it in his. She had strong fingers and soft, soft skin. "Are you here with a date?"

"I came with my father."

"I can't tell you how glad I am to hear that."

His voice was low and charming and wrapped around her with an intimacy that shut out the crowd around them.

The man was pure danger—a type of danger she wasn't used to. To have an impact, he didn't have to do much except just *be*. His smiles could be perilous, his touch hazardous. He had the ability to make a woman's knees weak and her heart vulnerable. She was sure there were quite a few women in the room jealous of her, but it didn't matter. She *had* to ignore both his polished come-on and the electric way he made her feel, as if she had come alive only when he'd walked across the room to her. She cleared her throat. "By the way, thank you for including my father."

He tilted his head, his gaze thoughtful. "Including him?"

"Inviting him here tonight."

"Of course."

His tone indicated that inviting her father had been a given, and because it did, he drew another smile from her. Funny how easy it was to smile at him when it should be the exact opposite. "There are people who don't think of inviting him once the work is completed," she explained. "So he really enjoys occasions like this."

"I'm *happy* to have both him and you here

tonight." He paused. "Is your mother here too?"

"My mother passed away six years ago."

"I'm sorry."

His sincerity touched her. The dark circles beneath his eyes made her curious. They cast intriguing shadows into the light brown depths.

The Degas girl glided up to him with a soda in a crystal glass on a silver tray. "Mr. Damaron?"

"Thank you." He took it and handed it to Jolie.

"Thank you," she murmured to the girl, whose face had fallen with disappointment. She waited until the girl had left, then said, "She wanted you to notice her."

His brow knitted. "Who?"

"The girl who brought the soda. She's very cute in her little tutu."

"Really?" It never occurred to him to look at the server. He couldn't tear his gaze away from Jolie. "You're beautiful."

The floor shifted beneath her. Coming from him, a man who had riveted her attention from the moment she'd seen his photograph in the newspaper, the compliment meant more than it should have. Steady, she told herself. She didn't want to be rude to him, but she needed to remain objective and calm and not allow the tidal wave of his force to sweep her away. Right, she thought with self-deprecating humor.

"Why," he asked softly, "have I never seen you before?"

The iced soda slid down her throat as she sipped. "Probably because I never moved into your line of vision before."

"Is that true?" he asked.

He was staring at her as if she'd just said the most unbelievable thing. Her reply had been purposefully light, but he seemed to have taken it very seriously. She couldn't help but laugh. "Yes, it's true. Why would you think it wasn't?"

"Because there's something that seems familiar about you."

Maybe it was the fact that her chest was tightening, or maybe it was his statement, but suddenly she felt discomfort. "We've never met before."

"I didn't think we had met—it would have been hard for me to forget—but I thought if you lived in the area, we might have—"

"No," she said definitely. She didn't know where the conversation was going, but it was better to stop it. "We've never even crossed each other's path."

"So you don't live in the area?"

"That would be rather hard to do since you and several members of your family own almost this entire area of the state of New York."

He reached out and touched a sensitive spot at the base of her neck. "Not all of it."

She caught her breath. "Most of it."

What was it about her that intrigued him so? Jonah wondered. In a room full of beautiful, available women, she was the one who had pulled him to her and kept him with her. And she hadn't tried. He was positive she didn't even want him paying attention to her. But he could find no motivation to leave. "Then where do you live?"

She shrugged. "North of here."

He chuckled. "Are you trying to be a woman of mystery?"

The mere idea seemed to amaze her. "Good heavens, no."

"Most women *try* to be mysterious. You do it effortlessly."

"I don't mean to," she murmured.

"I know. It's what makes it so effective."

Her eyes had begun to water moments before, and now they were itching. "Do you have a dog?"

He laughed at the abrupt change of subject. "No. I don't have any pets. I love animals, but up to now I've traveled too much for it to be fair to have any."

Curiosity gained the upper hand over caution. "Up to now?"

"My plans are indefinite at the moment, but I'll probably be home for a while." He brushed his fingers over a silky strand of hair that lay across her brow. "Why did you ask if I had a dog?"

She thought about shrugging the question off, but decided there was no reason to. "I'm having the beginnings of an allergy attack. And as far as I know, the only thing I'm allergic to is dogs."

Instantly concerned, he whipped out his handkerchief. "Would this be of use?"

She took it, unsure what she was going to do with it. But it gave her something to hold on to. She hoped she wouldn't need it. "Thank you."

She'd learned over the years that her attacks were accelerated by heightened emotions. The heightened emotions that came into play when she was breaking into a stranger's home, stealing their family's art. And now, she was learning, her attacks could also be accelerated by the heightened emotions of being the focus of Jonah Damaron's attention.

"Jonah, wonderful party! Wonderful collection!"

Jolie tensed, hearing the familiar male voice.

"And how did you *ever* coax this amazing girl out to your party? Jolie, my dear, how exceptionally wonderful to see you!"

With real dread Jolie turned to see Winston Blakely approaching. An older man with a mane of silver hair and a dignified bearing, he owned a small, exclusive gallery in the city, which carried her work, when she allowed it. "Hello, Winston."

He bent to kiss both her cheeks. "You're here because of your father, of course." He turned to Jonah. "But it's still a coup to have this child. I've tried to get her to parties before, but she always claims shyness."

Jonah looked at her. "Shyness?" No, he didn't buy it. More than likely she didn't want the attention. And he found himself in the untenable position of wanting to do nothing but lavish attention on her.

"Thank you for sharing, Winston," she said wryly. "I can't tell you how happy it makes me."

"Bah! If I had my way, you'd be the toast of New York."

She felt like toast, period, she thought. *Burned.* Jonah had a way of looking at her that made her feel as if he already knew everything there was to know about her. Any additional knowledge Winston might give him would make her feel as if she had no skin.

Jonah's gaze went from one to the other. "How do you know each other?"

"You're not aware?" Winston asked, his shock apparent. "Jolie is an artist of great talent."

Jonah's eyes narrowed with interest. "I

didn't know. Jolie and I have just met and she hadn't gotten around to telling me." His voice dropped, but there was no mistaking the thread of humor. "But you would have soon, wouldn't you, Jolie?"

No, she thought. She wouldn't have. Remaining as anonymous as possible had always seemed like a good idea to her, especially to those people from whom she planned to steal. "We're standing in a room full of masters. I don't even begin to compare. What I do is nothing."

"Nonsense," Winston proclaimed. "You are every bit as unique an artist as the masters were in their time."

She barely managed to keep from snapping at him. "I plan to come into the city tomorrow, Winston. Perhaps we could speak then." As a brush-off, she knew it was pitiful, but she had to try something.

"Splendid. I'll treat you to lunch. Are you bringing me more work?" To Jonah, he said, "Jolie's work sells very fast, but she's remarkably stingy with it."

Please shut up, she thought, unconsciously pressing her hand against her chest. "I may bring something. I don't know." She'd made up the trip on the spur of the moment. How did she know what she would bring or not bring?

Jonah's expression was thoughtful. "I'd love to see your work, Jolie."

"*Winston!* How could I have not known you were here?"

Delight wreathed the older man's face as he spied the remarkable-looking redheaded woman approaching, red silk foaming around her like waves, her empty, jeweled cigarette holder waving in the air. "Abigail, my love! I was looking for you, but then I got sidetracked."

Her eyes dancing with merriment, she offered her cheek for a kiss. "I do believe I'm insulted."

"I'll make it up to you. Let me take you out for a late dinner."

The empty cigarette holder sliced the air. "I don't know. I'll have to play hard to get for a while before I decide." She turned to Jolie. "Jonah, darling, introduce me."

"I beg your pardon, Abigail. Abigail, this is Jolie Lanier. Her father, Colbert Lanier, restored two of the Matisse landscapes and the small Renoir. Jolie, this is my great-aunt, Abigail Damaron."

"And Jolie is a brilliant artist herself," Winston added.

Jolie stifled a groan and nodded to the older woman. "It's very nice to meet you, Mrs. Damaron."

Abigail took one look at her and said, "My dear child, you don't look as if you feel well."

"No, I don't." Abigail's astute observation gave her the break she needed. "Excuse me," she murmured. "I need to have a word with my father."

More than anything she simply wanted to get away from Jonah. As bad as she felt, she didn't plan to ask her father to leave the party to take her home. He was having too good a time. One way or the other, she decided, she could make it a little longer.

When her father saw her coming toward him, he held out his hand with a beaming smile. "I'm so glad you came over. You're missing the wonderful compliments on the paintings."

"I've seen all the people gathered around you. It's obvious your work is a great hit."

"Yes, it is. Everyone has been very impressed." He nodded to a passing couple. "You were speaking with Jonah Damaron? What did you think of him?"

There was no way one word could describe the man, but she picked the first one that came to her mind. "Nice."

The word reverberated through her mind. She couldn't believe she had chosen *nice* to describe him. Sexy. Dangerous. Charming. He was all of those things. But *nice*?

"That's what I thought," her father said. "I

met him briefly. He came over to personally thank me."

"Papa."

"What?" He frowned as he finally focused on her. "Are you feeling all right?"

"Not really."

"But there are no dogs around."

"Yes, I know. I'm not sure what I'm having a reaction to."

"Do you want to leave?"

Even though he had asked the question, she could already see the disappointment forming in his eyes. "Not yet. I think I'll try getting some air and see if that helps."

"Wonderful idea."

She wiped at her eyes with Jonah's handkerchief. As she did, she caught a whiff of his scent. The handkerchief smelled exactly like him, she realized. Masculine. Sexual. Disturbing. Distracted, she turned toward the Renoir. Her gaze fell on the bottom right-hand corner of the painting. Slowly her gaze cleared. And she froze.

Beside her she heard her father say, "Mr. Damaron, your party is a great success."

"Please call me Jonah, Mr. Lanier. I'd like you to meet my great-aunt, Abigail Damaron."

"Charmed. And you *must* call me Abigail. Every handsome man in the room does and so must you. I won't have it any other way."

Her father laughed, obviously pleased. "Then I most certainly shall."

"What's wrong?" Jonah asked softly.

He was behind her. She recognized his scent and she could feel the warmth of his body. She glanced around. "Nothing. Excuse me. I need to get some air."

THREE

Jolie grasped the concrete balustrade of the back terrace as she struggled for breath. She'd feel better now. It had been too hot in the salon, too crowded. And she'd been under too much stress.

Jonah Damaron. Winston Blakely. Her father. The Renoir.

No *wonder* she liked to stay home, she thought ruefully. It was safer there, comfortable.

Looking around, she spied a cushioned glider and collapsed into it. From there, she could hear the jazz being played by a quartet inside the salon—impressionistic music played for Impressionist art. It floated out into the night. The air was cool and crisp, the fabric cushions she sat on soft. The terrace lighting was subdued, not as bright as in the salon, easier on her currently stinging eyes. She would be all right now, she told herself again, and tried her best to relax.

Experimenting, she attempted to draw in a deep breath and managed a shallow one. Okay, she thought. A shallow breath was better than none.

Her bare arms were chilled, but her skin was flushed with heat. Briefly she closed her eyes. Lord, she *hated* her attacks. They pointed up to her the fact that no matter what she thought or wished, she was vulnerable and not as in control as she would like. She'd patterned her life so that the risk of the allergy attacks was limited. Unfortunately something that was outside her control tonight had happened. She wished she knew what.

Jonah Damaron. He sat down beside her, sending the glider swaying back and forth and her heartbeat speeding. "I brought you some water," he said, holding a crystal glass out to her.

"Stop." The one word was choked out.

"What?" he asked anxiously.

She pressed a hand to her aching chest and spoke from between clenched teeth. "Make . . . the glider . . . stop. . . ."

The glider instantly stilled. "I'm sorry," he said quietly. "What else can I do?"

"Nothing. I'm better." And she *had* been feeling better. But now . . . Was it the fact that her heart was racing that was making her chest hurt worse?

He held out the water to her. Carefully she leaned toward him to sip, thankful that he kept hold of the glass. She couldn't have guaranteed that she wouldn't drop what looked to be a very expensive piece of crystal. The liquid lubricated her dry throat, but her muscles were so tight it hurt to swallow.

"You should . . . go back to your guests," she managed.

"They're content and happy. They've got the paintings, plenty of food and champagne, and each other to talk to. They don't need me."

As much as she didn't like to admit it, she was glad he had followed her. She didn't know him well enough to be comfortable with him, but somehow she was reassured by his presence. "Thank you for coming out to check on me," she murmured. "It's not a lot of fun having one of these attacks by myself." And since the attacks usually happened only when she was busy breaking into people's homes, she was always alone.

"I'll take you to the hospital. Just say the word."

His voice was low and calm, but she could hear his concern and was comforted.

"No, I've got my medications. If I don't get better soon, I'll take them."

"Take them now." His eyes blazed at her as they had in the photograph.

She smiled weakly at his adamancy. "I'm stubborn. I always think I can beat this on my own . . . but you're right." She pulled the inhaler from her purse and took two quick blasts from it.

He watched her carefully. "How long before you'll feel better?"

"Ten minutes or so." She glanced at him and saw his brow knit worriedly. Truthfully she would probably get better faster if he wasn't hovering by her side. She'd already admitted to herself that heightened emotions didn't begin to cover how she reacted to his presence. But at the same time she didn't want him to leave.

"You must be very proud . . . of your collection," she said in an effort to get her mind off the fact that she was having more and more trouble breathing. "It's absolutely remarkable."

"Yes," he said, keeping a cautious eye on her. He hated listening to her wheeze as she struggled to breathe. And he hated not knowing how to help her. Inaction in a crisis was foreign to him and his mind was racing. Still he continued to talk, because he knew she wanted him to. "But I've never really considered it *my* collection. My father and mother accumulated it, piece by piece, buying only what they liked. It's a very personal collection and each painting has its own memories for me." As he spoke he watched her closely, trying to gauge what he should do. "When, where, how my parents came to discover and purchase each painting. What the occasion was, the circumstance."

She managed a small smile at him to let him know she was following what he was saying.

He held the water out to her. "More?"

"No."

"Are you cold?" Even as he asked he shrugged out of his jacket and put it around her. At least it was something he could do.

She gave a brief shake of her head. "Keep talking."

"The collection is going out on tour in their honor." He paused. Her hand had a death grip on the arm of the glider. Red splotches bloomed one after the other on her skin. "God, Jolie, there's got to be something I can do for you."

She could barely breathe, and at that moment she finally faced up to the fact that she wasn't getting any better. Quite the contrary. She looked at him and tears of helplessness spilled from her eyes and down her cheeks. She reached out for his hand, and when he took hers, she held on to him for dear life.

In that instant he saw what was happening, saw her fear, her panic. She was in trouble. And suddenly something clicked in his brain. Swearing violently, he tore the jacket from around her and swept her up into his arms.

She had no idea where they were going, but she clung to him. He was solid, while she was breaking up into pieces.

Eating up distances with long strides, he carried her up an outside rear staircase to a balcony and into a large, darkened room. A thousand thoughts were running through her mind, but none of them made any sense.

"Hang on, Jolie," he muttered. "Just hang on."

The inhaler should have helped.

"This is all my fault."

Where was he taking her?

"God, I should have realized—"

She needed the inhaler, the antihistamines. She needed to tell him.

"I'm so sorry."

She was going to die if she couldn't breathe.

"We're nearly there."

What was he saying?

She felt herself lowered onto something. Jonah left her, but then was back, lifting her onto his lap.

"This should help."

Steam filled up the room quickly. She realized they were in a bathroom, and he had turned on the shower.

"I've been meaning to have a steam room installed, but this is going to have to do for now."

He kept a firm hold on her with an arm around her waist while his other hand was between her shoulder blades, gently rubbing. His voice was soothing, though she still couldn't catch what he was saying. But she could hear the tone of his voice, hear his worry, and she had the vague wish that she could reassure him.

She'd never tried steam before, so she wasn't sure if it would help or not, but she leaned against him and laid her head on his shoulder. For now it was easier to use his strength; she had none.

"That's it," he crooned. "Take it easy. Don't struggle. Let the steam do its work."

She gripped his forearm with her hands and allowed his voice to comfort her. *He* comforted her. And she didn't have the strength or the breath to argue with him anyway. She concentrated on trying to relax.

"You're going to be all right," he said softly. "I won't have it any other way."

Her mind was slowly clearing now, and she would have smiled if she'd been able to. He'd sounded so certain of his abilities to make her better. How wonderful to have such assurance in yourself.

"Purse." As hard as the one word was to say, she wouldn't have been able to say it at all a minute ago.

"Purse? You want your purse? Oh, damn, I *forgot*. It has your medicine in it. I'll be right back."

He gently shifted her so that she was sitting alone, but true to his word, he quickly returned.

"Someone will bring it up immediately," he said, scooping her up again and sitting down with her in his arms.

"You don't . . . have to hold me."

"Hush." She felt incredibly frail in his arms and he didn't want to relinquish her just yet. He couldn't forget her fear and panic. The sight of those emotions in her eyes had hit him hard. "God, Jolie, I'm so sorry."

"Why?"

He put his hand along her jawline and eased her face up so that he could study her. "You asked me if I had any dogs. I don't, but an hour before the party began I was over at my cousin's, playing with his daughter and her dog. My jacket is probably covered in dog hairs and I put it around your shoulders. I'm very sorry, Jolie. I did just about everything wrong. I even left your purse with your medicine in it downstairs."

She shook her head. "Don't—"

The bathroom door opened and an older man entered and handed her the purse. "Anything else, Mr. Damaron?"

"Yes, tell Sin where I am. Tell him everything's fine and I'll be back down in a bit."

"Yes, sir, I'll be happy to." He left, shutting the door behind him.

She retrieved her inhaler and helped herself to a couple of blasts.

"What else can you do to help yourself?" he asked, watching her attentively. "Or what can I do?"

"You've already helped." Slowly she pushed against him and straightened. For a moment she remained still, making sure she wasn't dizzy. "I need to get out of here. Too much moisture is probably not good—"

Before she could say anything else, she was in his arms and out the door into the next room.

He deposited her on a bed, switched on a nearby light, then stood back, eyeing her anxiously. "What else?"

If she'd had the strength, she might have laughed. Having her wishes translated to reality, and so quickly, was new to her. "Water?"

In mere moments the water appeared. She took two antihistamines with it, then handed the glass back to him. He was standing in front of her as if he was afraid she would fall off the bed onto her face. She rummaged in her purse for the hard candy she was never without and slipped it into her mouth.

Then she took stock of herself. She'd lost her shoes somewhere. Her dress was still on and in place—that was something. But her hair had to be a mess, and her eyes and face probably looked as if she had some dreaded disease.

"I should warn you." She paused to carefully draw in a bolstering breath. "I may start talking very fast . . . and telling you all kinds of things . . . or I may crash and fall asleep. It'll be the medication—I never know."

He smiled briefly. "For purely selfish reasons, I hope it's the former, but either is fine with me. What I *don't* want is to ever again see you struggling like that for breath."

She sucked on the candy. "Sorry I gave you such a scare . . . and put you to so much trouble, but I'm going to be fine now."

"I hope so."

He looked decidedly skeptical and she couldn't blame him. It must have been extremely hard on him not knowing what was happening and having to go through one of her attacks with her. But he hadn't lost his cool. He had acted fast, and through it all he'd been incredibly gentle. She was very grateful to him, but she was also more than a little unnerved that he had seen her at her most vulnerable.

"Don't feel bad about causing my attack. You had no way of knowing."

He drew up a chair close to the bed, close to her, and sat down. "You asked me about dogs. The question should have rung an alarm bell with me." He smiled and this time the smile stayed. "I guess I was distracted."

She could tell she was better because she was once again aware of him as a man instead of as someone who was helping her. He was wearing a crisp, snow-white shirt that was in startling contrast to his bronze skin. The refinement of his pearl, onyx, and gold cuff links was also a contrast to the size, strength, and capability of his hands.

As she watched he began to slip the cuff links from the cuffs. "I've been very high-maintenance tonight. Please—go back to your guests."

"My guests are fine."

She was in a very large bedroom, she realized. "Is this your room?"

He nodded. "It's mine, even though I don't think I've spent more than three or four nights here in the past year and no two nights in a row." He tossed his cuff links onto the bedside table.

It seemed an intimate gesture, his taking

things off he'd been wearing. The attack had
unwound her usually tightly wound defenses.
She'd be back to normal soon, though. "It
must be exciting to travel as much as you do."

"It gets tiring," he said, lounging back in
the chair. "I'm happy to be home."

In the pool of light his eyes appeared dark,
his emotions hidden. One by one he rolled the
white sleeves up his arms, exposing the fine
black hairs growing across his forearms and the
muscles that lay beneath. He had carried her
up a staircase as if she were no more than a
feather. He had said he was happy to be home.
She was on his bed. . . .

What was she doing? He had just given her a
piece of information and she had nearly missed
it. Now *she* was the one who was distracted.
"So you're going to be staying here?"

"I think so."

"Wait. You already said that, didn't you?
You said your plans were indefinite, but you
would probably stay awhile."

He had had women cross entire continents
to be with him, some had even flown around
the world just to spend one night with him, yet
he said, "I'm flattered. You remembered what I
said." And he meant it.

"How long do you think you'll stay? How
long is awhile?"

"I'm not sure yet. Why?"

She shrugged. "No reason." She had given

Jonah Damaron enough to be curious about tonight.

He eyed her thoughtfully. "I just realized something. I should finish getting undressed."

After all she'd been through this evening, she would have thought she was beyond reacting to him in an emphatically physical way, but her heart thudded against her rib cage at his casually spoken remark. "Undressed?"

"If the dog hairs were on my jacket, they'll be on my pants and shirt. I'll be right back." He stood up, then hesitated. "Will you be all right alone for a few minutes?"

She nodded. "Yes."

"And you won't move?"

She smiled faintly. "I doubt if I could."

"Good. Stay put and I won't be long."

After he had left the room, she eased around on the bed and propped her back against the carved mahogany headboard. By the time he came back, she thought, her system would be in better shape and she'd be able to handle the jolting impact he had on her.

She closed her eyes and drew in a deep breath. It felt wonderful. She still felt shaky, too shaky to get up and rejoin the party, or to try to go home. But in another thirty minutes or so she should be able to.

Faintly she heard the music from the party, but it was only because Jonah had left the bedroom door to the balcony open. The house was sturdily built with thick walls. When he wanted to, she was sure he could seal the house up tight, without leaving so much as a crack through which someone like her, someone who planned to rob him, could slip.

She heard the shower. Unbidden, an image of what he must look like naked, standing beneath the shower, sprang into her mind. She could see the long muscled lines of him in her mind's eye as he stood beneath the shower, the water sluicing over him.

Her eyes flew open. This was no good. If she wasn't careful, she'd bring on another attack, this time a heart attack. And just as she was thinking that he walked back into the room, a towel draped around his shoulders, wearing a fresh pair of slacks and nothing else. Water glistened in the dark curling hair of his chest and hard, muscled abdomen, and she almost *did* have a heart attack.

Pressing a comforting hand to her chest, she glanced at the phone. "Can I get my father on that phone?"

He slid the towel off and sent it winging across the room. "Piece of cake. You want me to send for him?"

She nodded. He reached for the phone, punched in two numbers, and when it was answered on the other end said, "Ask Colbert

Lanier if he would come up to my room, please. His daughter would like to speak with him." Hanging up, he said to her, "Anything else?"

She laughed and almost choked doing it. "It's amazing how fast you can get something done."

"Most things."

The door opened and Sinclair Damaron strolled in, darkly sophisticated and elegant in an impeccably cut black evening suit, his dark jade eyes taking in the situation at a glance. "I got your message and thought I'd come up. Reynolds said a young woman was having an allergy attack. Can I do anything?"

"The young woman is much better," Jonah drawled, his gaze steady on her. "I, however, am a wreck." He winked at her. "Jolie, this is my cousin Sinclair."

His wink was so unexpected, she flushed. Great, she thought, ruefully. Every woman's dream was to be flushed and splotched and caught in an intimate scene with two very handsome men. Sinclair Damaron, however, didn't seem the least bit shocked or surprised to find her on his cousin's bed, with Jonah wearing only a pair of slacks. "Hi," she said, because she could think of nothing else to say.

"Are you sure you're okay?" he asked, his gaze as laser intense as Jonah's could be.

She nodded mutely.

"How's the party going?" Jonah asked his cousin.

"Great. The collection is going to be a big hit if the response downstairs is anything to go by. But then we knew that."

"My feet are killing me!" Abigail Damaron announced dramatically, surging into the room, brightly colored and energetic. "Are we gossiping about the guests downstairs? Is that what we're doing? How wonderful! And just in time, too, because I was getting bored." She sat down on the side of the bed and immediately turned her formidable attention to Jolie. "My dear, are you feeling any better?"

"Some." Jolie's response was as weak and overwhelmed as she felt.

"Jolie Christiane, how are you?"

This time it was her father coming through the door. She could have cried with relief. At last someone she knew. But before she could say anything, Jonah answered for her.

"She's doing much better. It was all my fault." He looked at Sin. "She's allergic to dogs and I had Kirby's hair all over my jacket." To her father, he said, "Kirby is my niece's dog."

"Ah." He looked at his daughter. "But you're better?"

"Yes, but I think I should go home now." She hated to take him away from what he viewed as his evening, but for many reasons that all seemed to involve Jonah, she didn't think it wise for her to stay. Besides, as nice as they were, the Damarons en masse were overpowering.

Her father leaned down and patted her hand. "Of course. I'll have the car brought around to the front and I'll be waiting for you."

Jonah's voice stopped Colbert Lanier halfway to the door. "I'm concerned about her traveling right now. It might be better if she spent the night here. Then you could enjoy the rest of the evening, Mr. Lanier, and I could take her home in the morning."

Her father was wavering, Jolie thought. The "enjoy the rest of the evening" part had gotten to him. She shook her head. "No, I—"

Abigail, who had been studying both Jonah and Jolie, spoke up. "I think that's an excellent idea, Colbert. Then you and I can close down the party, perhaps even go for a drive, stop for breakfast somewhere, watch the sun come up." She rose to her feet, went to his side, and laid her red-painted nails on his arm. "Please say you'll come with me, Colbert. You'll be helping me stand up another date. It'll be great fun."

With a sinking heart, Jolie watched her father's eyes light up. "It sounds wonderful, but . . ." He looked at her. "It's up to you, sweetheart."

Her gaze went to Jonah. He was smiling. She wanted very much to go home, to sleep in her own bed, to forget how embarrassed she was to be the center of attention of the powerful Damarons, and most of all to be the sole focus of *one* of them in particular. Jonah, the man with shadows beneath his eyes and both gentleness and strength in his hands.

"Stay," he said softly. "I'm worried about you."

To her chagrin, she felt a warmth melt through her.

Abigail sliced her cigarette holder through the air, her blue eyes twinkling magnificently. "You'll make an old woman very happy, Jolie. I can flirt the night away with your father, and all the while he'll know that you'll be well taken care of. It's a very good arrangement all the way around."

Jolie doubted that too many people ever told any of the Damarons no, but she would have—except for one thing. Jonah's offer to let her stay the night in his house was too good an opportunity to pass up.

The paintings she planned to steal within the next month were here. She could use the time to find out what she could about his security, the "layers" he had in place that would give her problems, and the layout. Then in the morning she'd leave.

She wouldn't see Jonah again. And when she was ready, she would be able to steal the paintings; no mess, no fuss.

Everyone would win. Everyone would be happy.

"All right," she said, and felt incredibly sad.

FOUR

The flame on the candle Jolie had lit wavered as she walked down the long hall of the second floor of Jonah's house. The antihistamines had hit her system hard, winding her up so tightly she felt she might jump out of her skin. Plus, she was in a strange house and had been given a strange bedroom to use as her own, with the disturbing Jonah Damaron just a few doors away. No, she definitely couldn't sleep.

Besides, she couldn't find out what she needed to know about the Damaron security system while she slept. The chance to obtain the information was the one reason she had agreed to stay.

The candlelight reflected off rich, dark paneling. Oriental carpets cushioned her bare feet. From what she could make out, it seemed a wonderful house, a house that had once been a home and was ready and eager to be a home again, even though the master of the house was apparently never there.

As she made her way downstairs and passed through room after room, hall after hall, she caught glimpses of family pictures and mementos that hung on the walls or that were set on shelves.

She had one main destination—the salon—but she kept getting sidetracked. Jonah, she discovered, had had a red tricycle when he was little, and a beat-up baseball cap that he wore in all of the pictures of him at that age. Later on in school, he had played football.

As a little boy, in torn jeans and a dirty T-shirt, riding his tricycle, his brown eyes flashed fierce delight. As a young man in his football uniform, with black smeared beneath his intensity-filled eyes, he looked like a young warrior. He hadn't changed much, she thought. Despite the gentleness with which he had helped her earlier, he still had the same fierceness, the same intensity.

What did he use it for, she wondered, now that there were no more tricycles to ride or school sports to excel in? What did he do with all that intensity and fierceness? All that passion? Because he had it. In spades.

The knowledge added to the jitteriness she felt.

She stopped at the arched entryway to the

long salon where the party had been held. Empty of people now, it was lit by intermittent, pale pools of light. But the room didn't need people to bring it to life. The paintings did that, each one breathtakingly brilliant in its own right. And here was a roomful of them.

She had a fine appreciation of art and she couldn't imagine what it must be like to own such treasures. But if she did, she would have a state-of-the-art security system to make sure they were kept safe, and Jonah, she was certain, would too.

"Is anything wrong?"

She started at the sound of Jonah's deep voice, brusque with a touch of alarm. Slowly she turned toward him. He still wore the slacks he had put on after the shower, but he had added a crisp white shirt. He hadn't buttoned it, though, and she had a clear view of his broad chest and the fine black hair that matted it. She couldn't decide which was sexier, him with no shirt, or him wearing a shirt he had casually thrown on. "Nothing's wrong."

"Then what are you doing here?" he asked, frowning. "Couldn't you sleep?"

She tried to keep her gaze focused on his face instead of allowing herself the luxury of visually exploring the enticing part of his muscular torso left bare by the open shirt. "I was having a little trouble."

"Is it your medication? You warned me it might wind you up."

"It did." The truth was, just being in his vicinity was stimulant enough to keep her awake. Unfortunately he had spoiled her chance to do some snooping, at least for now.

He smiled. "Does that mean that you're about to tell me all kinds of things?"

The blatant gleam of masculine appreciation in his golden brown eyes captured and held her attention. He made her acutely aware that she was wearing only a man's shirt with panties beneath it. She barely resisted the urge to tug on the shirt's hem, to double-check that she was adequately covered. "Things?"

"That's what you told me. You said the antihistamines would either make you sleep or wind you up and make you tell me all kinds of things."

She remembered. "It's true. Sometimes the antihistamines trip something in my brain and I have trouble focusing on one thing. When that happens, I've been known to talk a blue streak."

"About yourself, I hope. You don't give much away."

She deliberately kept her response light. "There's not too much to tell. And as for how I'll react, I never know." The reaction she was having now was very strange. Her nerves were sparking like Fourth of July firecrackers, but she wasn't talking particularly fast. She was however having trouble keeping control of her train of thought. She should be concentrating on business rather than trying to fight the urge to press her hands to his chest and delve her fingers through the dark curling hair.

His expression loaded with interest, he folded his arms across his chest. "I'm waiting."

Amused, she shook her head. "You know, I have to compliment you."

"You *have* to? Does that mean you don't want to, but will anyway because you have no choice?"

She chuckled and was surprised to hear the sound coming from her. He was too easy to be with, too easy to talk to. She had to remember that all those sharp angles of his could cut and slice. "I always have a choice."

"Then I'm glad your choice tonight was to stay."

"Jonah," she said wryly. "If you want to hear a compliment, you're going to have to refrain from asking another question or interjecting another subject into the conversation."

His brows shot up, but he replied mildly, "Then I'll be quiet because I want to hear it."

A small thrill shivered through her at the easy way he had taken her ultimatum. She only had to look at him to know that he wasn't a man accustomed to yielding to anyone. "I simply want to say that you've been remarkably good-natured about this whole thing. First you found yourself with a woman on your hands who couldn't breathe, and now you find the same woman in the middle of the night, wandering around your house, high on antihistamines."

"I was glad I was there for you when you couldn't breathe. As for the latter, believe me, it's my pleasure. And in either case, as long as the woman is you, I'm very happy. And by the way, I like the phrase you used, a woman on my hands."

He stepped closer to her. Or did he? It could have been her reaction to his words, but whatever it was, her skin actually warmed and her senses came tinglingly alive at his clean, masculine smell. "What about you?" she asked, her voice huskier than normal. "Couldn't you sleep?"

"It's been a long time since I've been able to fall asleep this early."

"It's two in the morning. That's late."

"Yes, it is, but I'll be up another couple of hours yet." Without elaborating further, he glanced into the salon. "Were you going in?"

"I wasn't sure I should."

"Why not?"

"I thought you might have some sort of security for the room and I could set it off if I barged in."

"Barge ahead. I haven't put it on yet."

She stifled a rueful sigh. A confirmation of something she'd already been sure of—that he had a security system for the room, for the house—was of little help to her.

"When *do* you usually arm the system?"

"It depends. Tonight I knew I was going to come back down here. It's a nice room to relax in."

He hadn't answered her—he had simply explained why he hadn't put the alarm on yet —and she wondered if it had been deliberate on his part. While she was planning what her next question would be, he surprised her by gesturing toward the shirt she was wearing. "It never looked that good on me."

"It's yours?" She glanced down at it. The white shirt ended at the middle of her thighs, she'd rolled the sleeves up to just below her elbows, and she'd left several buttons open at the top. Self-consciously she smoothed her hand down her side, feeling the softness of the fabric. It was that softness that had made her choose it over the gowns and pajamas she had found in the room.

He nodded. "Used to be a favorite actually. I wore it a lot." He ran his palm down one of its sleeves, stroking her arm in the process. "I can't remember the last time I saw it—must be years. Where did you find it?"

"In one of the drawers of the big cherrywood chest." He nodded as if he knew exactly which chest she was talking about and she wondered if he really did. He'd said he'd been home only three or four nights during the past year. Still he didn't strike her as a man who was careless with his things. All the more reason for her to proceed with caution. "If you haven't seen this shirt in years, how do you know it's yours?"

He reached out to grasp the collar and folded it backward so that he could see its inside. When he did, the material shifted, scraping her nipples, making them tingle. Then again, just his nearness had the very same effect on her.

"It's embroidered," he said. "JLD."

"Embroidered?"

"I never liked monograms, but my mother believed in monograms. We compromised." He released the collar.

The material fell back into place, once again sliding over her breasts, bringing her nipples to an even more sensitive state. She forced her mind off the sensation and back to what they had been talking about.

Because of the family pictures she'd seen on the walls, she had no difficulty envisioning him as younger. He would have adored his mother. She could even imagine the good-natured conversation they must have had when they decided to compromise.

She passed a hand over her face. Good

Lord. She needed to get out of this house and away from him. She was becoming way too involved.

"If you want to see the initials for yourself," he murmured, "you can take the shirt off."

He *was* closer, *much* closer. And it was impossible to stand this close to him without feeling the impact of his male sexuality. It was forceful, heated, controlled, ever seducing, drawing a woman nearer and nearer whether she wanted to go or not. She tried to keep her tone light. "Well, now there's a tempting suggestion."

"It is to me."

"Tempting, but not necessary. I believe you. JLD?"

"Jonah Lionel Damaron. Lionel is a family name."

"Did anyone ever call you Lion?"

"No. There's another Lion in our family. He'll be in the city tomorrow if you'd like to meet him."

"No thank you." She'd met enough Damarons to last her a lifetime. And even if she hadn't met any of them but Jonah, she would still feel the same way. He had a presence that filled up spaces and . . . minds. As he had done hers. Since she'd met him earlier in the evening, he had completely dominated her thoughts and many of her reactions.

She moved away from him, stiffer than she would have liked, and entered the salon. "There are all sorts of clothes and things in the guest room," she said, having searched for and finally settled on a neutral topic of conversation.

The furniture, she noted, had been moved back into the salon. There were couches and chairs upholstered in damask and velvets, the fabrics obviously well-worn, and there were tables ladened with more family mementos and pictures. The room obviously hadn't been redecorated in years. Amazingly, as big as the room was, and as public as it had obviously been designed to be, with the museum-quality masterpieces hanging on the walls, it was still a cozy room.

Without the paintings, and despite its size, it looked like any other living room. Yes, she was sure his mother had chosen everything in the room. With one phone call he could have had the room redone at any time, and she was strangely touched that he hadn't.

She looked around and found Jonah still standing in the doorway, watching her. "There's anything in the guest room you'd want, really," she said, continuing with the thread of conversation she had started. "You must have a lot of guests."

"Over the years, but not lately."

She strolled from painting to painting, but

didn't linger at any single one. For one thing, the lighting wasn't good enough for close study. But most of all she couldn't concentrate on even a great master with Jonah watching her. It took a lot of emotional energy to be with him, to resist him. And she was very afraid it was going to take even more energy to leave him in the morning.

He'd left the doorway and entered the room, effectively reducing its size in her mind. She had the option of going back to the guest room, but once there, she'd probably just pace. And there, she couldn't learn anything that might be useful. Here, she still had a chance.

She placed the candle she'd been carrying on a side table, then sat down in the corner of a green velvet sofa. Studiously ignoring another very important reason she didn't want to go back upstairs—there, she'd be alone—she said, "But the things in the guest bedroom, the clothes . . ."

"The items there are either things we've provided for overnight guests or things guests have left behind."

She gazed at him. Shadows and light played across his face, making him appear even harder and more enigmatic than she guessed him to be. Yet he had been nothing but nice to her. She should quit bringing up inconsequential subjects. She should concentrate on getting information. But whether it was the medication or the pull he was exerting on her senses, she couldn't resist talking to him about something that would be of no help to her on the night she came to break into his house and rob him.

"Apparently you've had some interesting guests. There's a black negligee in the closet with about a foot of lace around the hem and sleeves. I tried to imagine whom it might belong to, but couldn't. Do you happen to know?"

"I don't have a clue." He moved to open one of the French doors, allowing the moonlight and fresh air to spill into the room. And with it came the fragrant scent of night-blooming flowers.

She savored the scent and reflected that he was being kind and tactful by not saying more to her. If a woman with a black negligee came to visit him, she'd stay in *his* room, not the guest room. And of course, he would take *off* the clothes of the woman to whom he was making love, not give her something to put *on*.

She suddenly knew without question that he would make love to a woman fiercely and intensely. The realization left her shaken.

He strolled back toward her, devastatingly attractive in the moonlight and shadows. "But I have to say, I'm sorry you didn't choose the negligee to wear instead of the shirt. I can only imagine how you would look in it."

He hadn't let her off scot-free after all. She

had to be more careful. *Smarter*. They weren't just *any* man and woman, exchanging banter. She'd known that earlier in the evening and she forcefully reminded herself of it now. She should stay as far away from him as possible. She had secrets to keep, laws to break. Yet here she was with him, in the middle of the night, wearing nothing but one of his shirts, in what was becoming an increasingly intimate situation. And her meandering thoughts weren't helping her.

Without warning, he leaned down to her, his mouth coming nearer and nearer to hers. Her heart ceased to beat. She forgot to breathe. She could see the pores of his skin, smell his clean, warm, musky scent. His full lips were slightly parted. He was going to kiss her and she was going to let him. In fact she was waiting for him to, anticipating how it would feel, the heat, the pressure.

She'd lost her senses, but apparently he hadn't. At the last moment he turned his head aside to blow out the candle beside her. She'd forgotten about it.

"You made a very romantic sight, carrying a candle," he murmured, still leaning over her, his face once again close to hers.

"I didn't want to bother anyone by turning on any lights."

"You wouldn't have."

He straightened away and she was instantly

aware of the disappointment she felt. But also thankful, very thankful. Kissing him would have been a detour for her and detours were always time-consuming, sometimes rough, and usually difficult to find your way back from.

She forced her mind back to the business at hand. "There's no one here?" Layers. An estate like this had to have layers protecting it.

"Does it make you nervous to think that we're here alone?"

Actually the knowledge electrified her, heightening sounds and senses. She was being drawn to the flame, and to make matters worse she was enjoying it. "Should it?"

"Questions." He laughed lightly and huskily. "The lady talks in questions."

"The middle question was yours. But to answer the last, no, it doesn't make me nervous."

He dropped down beside her, so close his thigh was touching hers. As he slid his arm along the back of the couch, his eyes gleamed. "What does make you nervous, Jolie?"

"You're getting off the subject."

"The subject?"

"Does anyone live on the estate?"

He stared at her for a moment. "You're really interested?"

"Chalk it up to curiosity. I don't live on an estate."

"But you won't tell me where you live."

"You told my father you'd take me home in the morning. You'll find out then."

"Yes, I will, won't I?"

He slowly smiled and she couldn't begin to guess what he was thinking. She never got involved with people from whom she planned to steal. Never. This man was supposed to be her prey, and instead he was preying on her, heating her insides, scrambling her thoughts.

"Okay," he said, "if you're really interested. A few people live on the property and a couple lives in an apartment in a small wing off the kitchen."

She still didn't know much more than she'd already surmised, but at least it was something.

"But we're basically alone," he added, and brought her attention back to him. "And I would like to think that it makes you at least a little nervous." His deep, dark voice lit sparks along her nerves. "In fact, it'd be very good for my ego if that were the case."

A slight smile curved her lips as she shook her head. "The vast majority of the women at the party tonight were salivating over you, Jonah, plus your other male cousins. You don't need me to stroke your ego."

His gaze dropped to her lips. "Maybe not my ego, but feel free to stroke any other part of me you'd like."

Oh, yes, he was charming, but that was part of his danger. There was a force in him she could feel pulling at her, even when he wasn't touching her. She was crazy to be talking to him like this. "Once again, Jonah, and against my better judgment, I'll point out that there were quite a few women in this very room tonight who would have loved for you to say something like that to them. You should have asked one of them to stay the night."

"I asked the woman I wanted."

Heat shuddered through her. She'd known it all along and he'd just reminded her—he was a man who would flirt and spar as long as it suited him, and then he would cut to the bottom line. She looked away, out the open doorway to the moonlit grounds beyond. It was a beautiful, ethereal scene. She had so much pent-up nervous energy, she could have danced the entire length of the grounds and back. In fact she wished she could. It might soothe her nerves.

"Would it be possible for me to get a glass of milk?"

His expression changed, became attentive in a different way. "Are you hungry? You didn't touch any of the hors d'oeuvres served tonight."

"How do you know?"

"I know," he said slowly and without even a trace of a smile, "because you were the most watchable person in the room tonight. I'll be right back with your milk."

He had been watching her. It took her a few moments to absorb that unsettling thought.

She had always been a private person, preferring to blend into the wallpaper rather than be on display. And she'd always been fairly successful at it. The idea that Jonah had been studying her without her being aware of it unnerved her. But then, what else was new? Against all common sense she was attracted to him. And she couldn't even begin to contemplate the ramifications of the fact that she desired him.

She had no idea how far the kitchen was from the salon, but as soon as she was able she jumped up and began circling the room, her eyes going to the obvious and then the not-so-obvious places where the security-system control panel would be located. Unfortunately she didn't see anything she hadn't already seen at the party. It wouldn't be impossible to break into the room, the house, but it was going to be damned hard.

She circled the room once more and was back sitting on the sofa when Jonah returned with a tall glass of milk. He handed it to her, then settled down beside her once again.

She drank several swallows of the milk before she spoke. "I've been thinking about your paintings."

"I'm disappointed. I've been thinking about you."

He was sidetracking her again, actually more like *derailing* her. Worse, she saw it coming, and was going to allow him to do it. She took another drink of the milk, then set it beside the candle on the side table. "Thinking *what* about me?"

"I've been wondering what it would feel like to kiss you."

Her breath caught in her throat and she struggled for control. The struggle was automatic. Truthfully and amazingly she didn't really want control. Not at this moment. Her life was incredibly disciplined, every moment with a purpose. The time she spent at her painting was the closest she came to self-indulgence, self-indulgence because she loved it so. But her paintings were also her livelihood and therefore not entirely without purpose.

Kissing Jonah would be a *true* indulgence. Without purpose. Without reason.

She nodded her head slightly and spoke barely above a whisper. "It would probably be very nice for both of us."

"Nice?" He lifted a hand and stroked his thumb across her bottom lip. "Yes, I think you're right, but on the off chance that you're wrong, I want to find out for myself." His gaze went to her lips, then returned to her face. "All right?"

He was asking permission, something she intuited he rarely did. It was her chance, maybe her *only* chance, to say no. "All right."

The pressure of his mouth on hers was firm, the feel warm, as he brushed his lips back and forth across hers. It was just as she'd expected, she thought. Nice, extremely nice. Lord, it was *more* than nice.

Either he had a great deal of experience at kissing or she was extremely responsive to him. Both, she suspected. As he pressed his mouth down on hers, shaping her lips, occasionally nipping, she found herself opening her mouth wider and softly moaning.

With his hands on her shoulders, he tugged her closer to him, and slipped his tongue deep into her mouth. Sweet heat wound through her, enticing, enthralling. Eagerly she met his tongue with hers and set about learning its texture, its taste. The heat turned to a simmering fire that flowed through her and down into her lower body.

She felt him shudder—or was that her?—and he increased the pressure of his hands on her, drawing her closer to him until finally her breasts were pressed against his chest, the stiffened nipples pushing against the soft cloth of the shirt, aching for relief. She flattened her hands against the muscled strength of his chest, her fingers finding the dark curly hair she'd fantasized about before. His chest was like an erotic playground she never wanted to leave. She suspected his body would be an entire amusement park. Her thoughts shocked her so much, her eyes flew open.

"You were wrong," he said with a husky groan. "Kissing you wasn't nice."

"No," she whispered in agreement. At the moment she couldn't think of an adequate word, and he didn't give her any more time to think.

His mouth came down on hers again, harder this time, his tongue thrusting deep into her mouth with more force. He found her breast through the soft shirt, taking it fully into his hand, caressing her and stroking her until she was squirming against him.

She felt him reach for the buttons on the shirt and begin to undo them one by one. And she was amazed at herself. The hot, needy person she had become after only a few kisses was a revelation to her.

His fingers brushed against the bare skin of her breasts as he undid another button and heat stabbed through her. Another second, another button undone, and she knew she would be lost. She broke off the kiss and bolted to her feet.

With a groan Jonah wiped a hand over his face, then sat back and watched as she moved toward the French doors, buttoning the shirt as she went. She walked with an unconscious grace, her golden-brown thighs firm, her long legs shapely. Her nipples pushed against the soft cotton of the shirt, still aroused. Just as he was.

She stopped by one of the opened doors. He could smell the scents of the fragrant gardens that lay beyond. He even thought he could smell her scent, a mysterious, feminine fragrance that beckoned to him.

He'd thought he knew what it would be like to kiss her, but he hadn't even come close in his estimation. More than that, he couldn't remember wanting a woman as much as he wanted her. And the truly amazing thing was, his feelings for her went beyond sex, even now when he was hard and aching for her.

He rubbed his hand over his face again, trying to clear his head so that he could analyze what he was feeling. From the first moment he had seen her, something about her had struck a familiar chord in him. It still did. But what was it?

He knew what it was like to lead a life of secrets and deceptions, where trust was a foreign concept and wariness was an everyday emotion. And he knew what it was like to make fear his best friend; it had saved him many times.

Was it possible that she possessed some of those very same traits? But if she did, why?

"What's wrong?" he asked quietly.

"Nothing."

"Did I do something you weren't ready for?"

"No. Yes." She looked at him. In this one thing, she'd be totally honest with him. "The problem was, I was *too* ready."

He found himself incapable of saying anything for a moment. Finally: "That's not the wisest thing you could have said right now."

"Yeah, I know. Look, I'm sorry. I think I either need to go up to the guest room alone, or we need to go back to talking."

"That's what you think, huh?"

"That's what I think."

He let out a long, strangely painful breath. "Okay, then what do you want to talk about?"

"Well—your paintings."

He didn't want to talk about the paintings. Hell, he didn't want to talk at all. He wanted to go to her, to drop with her to the floor and take her there, in the moonlight, in the fragrance, and keep her in his arms all night long.

But he'd go along with her. For now. Because he wasn't ready for her to disappear to her room. And he wasn't ready to be alone with only the paintings and the night and the fragrance. "What about them?"

She took a few steps back toward him, then clasped her hands in front of her. "I was wondering if you were going to miss them when they go out on tour."

"Of course. They're a part of my life."

Her brow furrowed as something tickled at her memory. "I remember you said that your parents had chosen each one for personal reasons."

"Yes, they did." He shifted, sliding his arms along the back of the sofa, trying to stretch the muscles and pacify his body, which wanted a different kind of relief. "Once my dad bought a Monet simply because of the wonderment he saw in my mother's face when she looked at it."

Her eyes widened. "What a very special thing for him to share with you."

"They were both unique people."

"Were? They're not living?"

"No."

He didn't elaborate and she thought it best not to question.

He went on. "I understand the monetary value of the paintings only too well, plus their cultural importance. But they also have another value for me, a private value that no one else will ever know. I don't have my parents anymore, but I have things they loved. It helps."

Guilt flared through her. "Yet you're going to send the paintings out on tour."

"I've had them all to myself for many years. I can share for a while."

"But you're home now and they'll be gone soon. What, in a month?"

"A couple of weeks. Bad timing, but they'll come back."

Two weeks. She had less time than she had thought. "And will you be here when they come back?" If he stayed home, in a place that had good memories for him, would the shadows fade away?

A soft smile touched his lips. "This is my home. I'll be here."

Almost unconsciously she drew nearer to him. She was asking questions the answers to which wouldn't help her in stealing from him. But those answers might help her learn more about him, something that was becoming more and more important to her. "Even if it's only four or five nights a year?"

"You never know."

She wouldn't be in his life after tonight. She wouldn't know when the paintings would come back to him. She wouldn't know when and if he'd sit here in this enormous room in the middle of the night with the paintings. Or whom he would sit with. "Why do you travel so much?"

"Family business. Now you tell me something. Why do you ask me so many questions about myself, but tell me nothing about yourself?"

She smiled. "Because I'm smart."

He patted the sofa cushion beside him. "Come sit down."

"I—"

"Please. There's something I want to tell you."

"What is it?"

There was that wariness. It never seemed to leave her. "I'll tell you . . . when you come sit down."

She did, without explanation or rationalization either to herself or to him. She came down close to him and angled toward him.

"You know," he said almost meditatively, "when I first saw you earlier tonight, I had a hard time looking at anyone or anything else. There was something about you that demanded my attention."

She was too startled by the admission not to ask, "What?"

"I'm still not sure." He slid his hand over her hair and down to her neck, where he let it rest, his strong brown fingers on the delicate cream satin of her skin. "I'll let you in on something. I've just come through several years of living life on the edge, of not being able to ever let my guard down. And I'm tired."

She couldn't help herself. She reached her hand to the shadows beneath his eyes and lightly touched them. "And that's the reason for these?"

"Probably." He took her hand and kissed the palm.

A thrill shot through her.

"I'm tired," he murmured, "and you are complicated as hell, aren't you?"

"Yes," she said softly. "So stay away from me."

"Why?"

"It's for the best." She rose from the couch. "And now I'm going up to the guest room."

"Why?"

"Because it's for the best."

FIVE

Jolie didn't expect to be able to sleep after she returned to the guest room. She felt so much energy when she was with Jonah, so many turbulent and conflicting emotions. She should have been up all night. But a lot had happened, physically and mentally, draining her, and her body had been hit hard by the allergy attack and the medications. As soon as she climbed into the four-poster bed and settled onto the feather mattress, she fell into a deep sleep, so deep that when she awoke hours later she was disoriented.

She lay there, staring at the sun streaming through unfamiliar windows and at a ceiling that she had never seen before, listening, but hearing nothing but quiet. Slowly it came back to her. The party. The allergy attack. Jonah—

the way he had taken care of her, the way he had kissed her. The way *she* had kissed *him*.

She still wasn't certain how she'd managed to have enough composure to walk away, when what she'd really wanted to do was stay with him and let whatever happened happen. But walking away had been for the best.

She showered in the rose-and-cream marble bath that adjoined the bedroom, then dressed again in the only piece of clothing she had with her, the long black gown she'd worn to the party. Her purse contained both a compact with pressed powder and a lipstick, but she didn't bother with either. Anxious to get home, she simply ran a comb through her hair, then ventured downstairs.

She was met by the older man who last night had retrieved her purse from the terrace and had brought it to the bathroom. "Good morning, Miss Lanier."

He didn't bow, but he gave the impression he did.

"Good morning. I'm sorry—you know my name but I'm afraid I don't know yours."

"Forgive me," he said, his expression kind, polite. "My name is Reynolds, and if you'll follow me, Mr. Damaron is in the morning room, having breakfast." He started off, but stopped and looked back at her in inquiry when he realized she hadn't moved.

Like the man for whom he worked, she observed wryly, he was obviously accustomed to people doing as he requested. "I was wondering if you could show me to a phone. I'd like to order a car."

"Oh, that won't be necessary. Mr. Damaron is planning to fly you home."

In one of the private helicopters parked on the side lawn of the house, she assumed. "But you see, *I'm* planning to take a car. So if you'd be so good as to—"

"Giving Reynolds trouble, are you, Jolie? And first thing in the morning too. Tsk, tsk."

She turned around to see Jonah lounging against the doorjamb, amusement glinting in his golden brown eyes.

"Shame on you," he said. "You've probably ruined his whole day."

"I'm sorry, Reynolds," she apologized because it seemed like the thing to say.

"It's quite all right, Miss Lanier," he said in a tone that told her he was sympathetic to her plight. To Jonah, he merely nodded.

But all of Jonah's attention was on her. "I'm taking you home, remember?"

The shadows were still there beneath his eyes, and she was barely able to resist reaching out to touch them as she had the night before. Had he slept? she wondered. "I decided I'd order a car and save you the trouble."

"That's very thoughtful of you, Jolie, but it's no trouble at all for me to take you home."

He straightened from the door and pressed a light kiss to her lips, then reached for her elbow and subtly urged her forward until she was walking beside him. "Right after breakfast."

He guided her into a room filled with sunshine, flowers, and the enticing aroma of coffee and fresh bread. She could have refused, but the lure of spending a few last minutes with him was too strong. So she took her place at the table, had toast and coffee, and savored the time.

An hour later he flew her home in his helicopter, with its rich black leather interior and high-tech soundproofing that enabled them to talk to each other without shouting. With her directing him, he landed in an empty field behind the rambling clapboard house where she had lived all her life, located at the end of a country road. He didn't switch off the engine, but he slid off the headphones he had been wearing and turned to her. "I'm due in the city for a board meeting within the hour, but I want to see you—"

"Then I won't keep you," she said, cutting him off before he could say more. This was where it ended for the two of them. Though he didn't know it, they had two distinctly different goals from this point on—he, to protect what was his; she, to break through that protection. "Thanks for the ride home. And . . . thank you for your help last night." She reached for the handle to open the door, but he put his hand on her arm.

"More than your allergy attack happened last night, Jolie."

She had hoped they could part neatly, without either of them bringing up those intimate moments they had shared in the night. In the light of day there was a danger of reading more into what had happened than there had actually been.

But she didn't duck the issue. "It's a new day and you and I need to go our separate ways."

"For a short while."

She shook her head. "Jonah, I don't think—"

He stretched across the space that separated them, slid his hand around the back of her neck, and brought her mouth to his for a kiss that shook her. When he finally lifted his head away, they were both breathing unevenly.

"Maybe it's better not to think," he muttered, his eyes shining with glints of steel that brooked no argument. "I'll see you soon."

"Very nice, indeed, Jolie!" her father called out as she entered the house by the back door and made her way into the kitchen. She found him standing by the sink, coffee cup in hand, staring out the window as Jonah's helicopter disappeared in the distance. "Very nice way to be brought home, my dear. The Damarons certainly don't do anything halfway, do they?"

"You tell me." She tossed her purse onto the table and headed for the coffeepot and her second cup of the day. "You were out with a Damaron last night."

"Ah, Abigail. What a charming woman! She stole my heart right away, she did."

Jolie paused with the cup midway to her lips to give her father a closer look. Was it possible he had actually fallen in love with Jonah's great-aunt? In her experience it took a lot to pull him out of himself. Yet she had met Abigail and he was right. She *was* charming.

"So tell me about Mr. Jonah Damaron," he said. "You obviously made a great hit with him. He was being very protective of you last night."

So much for his attention being captured by Abigail, she thought, amused, and set out to defuse whatever he might be thinking about her and Jonah. "He was simply being a concerned host, that's all. It was very nice of him to let me stay the night."

"Yes, yes, it was. And what a grand art collection he owns," he said, his tone as close to rapturous as she ever heard it. It was the art, always the art, that he cared about.

"Yes, well, it's currently three paintings *less* grand than it was." She pulled out a chair from the table and dropped onto it. She wasn't looking forward to the conversation she was about to have with him, but it was very necessary. "Sit down, Papa. I need to talk with you about something."

"Not now. I must get to my painting—"

"*Now*, Papa. Please."

His eyes widened at her sharp tone. "What is it, Jolie Christiane? You are all right, aren't you?"

"Yes, I'm fine."

"Then what—"

"Please, could you just sit down for a minute?" She was physically rested, but the subject she was about to discuss with her father made her immensely weary. It was a subject she had discussed with him many times, but with no satisfying resolution. This time she had to find some way to prevail, to get him to see the way things really were, instead of the way they were in his mind. She waited until he had taken the seat across from her. "I got a good look at the Renoir you restored. Or rather your forgery of the Renoir that is now hanging in the Damaron salon."

He beamed. "Magnificent, isn't it? One of my best."

"Papa, you made a mistake—I saw it almost instantly—in the bottom right-hand corner."

He waved his hand and shook his head at

the same time. "No, no, my dear. You are wrong. There is no mistake on that painting."

"I'm not wrong, Papa. I know Renoir's brush strokes. You made a mistake."

"No," he said, again shaking his head, this time harder. "Remember, you were having an attack at the time. Your usually excellent discernment was obviously impaired. Yes, that was it."

"You're probably right," she said, remembering her uncharacteristic reaction to Jonah. "And if you are right, then I'm all the more alarmed, because the mistake was very obvious to me."

He picked up a knife from the table and fretfully tapped it against the butter dish. "My hand is as sure as it ever was. So is my eye. There is no one better than I am. No one."

She sighed. "Papa, listen to me, *really* listen to me. I've told you many times before that forging masterpieces and passing off your work as the real thing is wrong."

He gave a dismissive wave of his hand. "Bah! No one gets hurt. Where's the harm?"

She tried to keep her voice level. "The harm is that when you get through doing your job, the owners of the masterpieces don't have the masterpieces any longer. What you do is *illegal*."

"But they have *my* work, which is just as good and most of the time even better."

She had tried ranting, raving, even crying. On this subject nothing had ever gotten through to her father. Since her mother's death he had become more and more detached from reality. He wasn't delusional. He was flat-out obsessed, and she had learned there was no arguing with an obsession, no showing reason to an obsession.

This time, however, she *had* to get through to him. "Okay, let's forget that part for a minute, forget what's right and what's wrong. Think of *yourself*. Your hands are becoming unsteady." She rushed on to forestall the objection she could see forming on his face. "Maybe it's not apparent to you right now, but it is happening. You're not invincible, Papa. You are as susceptible to the problems of old age as anyone."

"I am *not* that old, Jolie Christiane, and I resent—"

Her hand came down on the table so hard the butter dish clattered and her father jumped. "If you continue to try to pass off your work as the genuine thing, you are going to get caught. And if you get caught, you *will* go to jail. Do you understand what I'm saying to you?"

"It won't happen. I'm too good."

She sighed. "You *were* good. But time is catching up with you." She raised her hand, palm toward him. "Don't say anything more right now. If you'll really give some thought to what I'm saying, you will come to the conclusion that I am right. Think about what Mama would have wanted you to do. Think about that really hard, and we'll talk more about this tomorrow."

Bringing up her mother was her trump card, and she could see from his expression that it had made an impression. Her mother had been the guiding light in his life, the one person who with a word or a smile could make him forget his art. She had been his consuming passion, and when she had died he had turned more and more to the art.

She rose and pressed a tender kiss to his forehead. "I'm going to change out of this dress, then I may go into the city. Winston Blakely was at the party last night and I said I'd go see him today. I'm thinking about doing it."

Her father nodded absentmindedly, having already retreated to a place in his mind where she barely existed. "That's nice," he murmured.

On impulse she hugged him. "I love you, Papa."

She could have called Winston with an excuse as to why she couldn't come to see him, but in the end she decided to go. She badly needed something to keep her occupied and she knew she wouldn't have been able to concentrate on her painting. So she dressed, tucking a white cotton T-shirt into a pair of beige linen slacks, threw a matching jacket over both, and took the train into New York City.

Years ago when she had first begun to view as a career what she had always done—create pictures on canvas with oil—she had approached Winston to see if he would be interested in carrying her work. His gallery hadn't been as exclusive then as it was now. Back then he carried new artists who had the talent but not the recognition. Over the years his astute picking and choosing of artists had stood him in good stead, and his gallery had grown in prestige in direct proportion to the growth in prestige of the artists he exhibited.

She couldn't take even partial credit for his success, however, since at the most she gave him only four or five of her paintings a year to sell.

He didn't understand. She supposed no one would understand. But the truth was, she had no wish to become well-known. She knew Winston thought her strange and eccentric, and he was absolutely right. But she couldn't help herself. The idea of becoming a household name made her cringe. It was instinctive and had something to do with her fear of being discovered. But if someone had asked what she was hiding, she'd have to say she wasn't sure.

Anything personal about her, she supposed. Anything that really mattered to her. Her father. And the things she did to protect her father.

She supposed some critical gene was missing from her makeup. Most people wanted to be well-known and make a lot of money. But she didn't need a lot of money to make her happy. She received satisfaction from the process of creating a painting, and so far that satisfaction had been enough for her.

Still, even though she had done very little to contribute to Winston's success, he had always treated her as if she were the most important artist he showed. And even though she was positive he treated all of his artists the same way, she appreciated his kindness. And shrewdness.

"My dear," he was saying now, "what can I do to entice you to come see me more often?"

They were in his office, having just returned from the lunch he had promised her. "Now, Winston, if I came any more often, you'd fuss at me that I wasn't spending enough time at my painting."

"I would never do such a thing." He placed his hand over his heart as if he were pledging. "*Never.*" His hand dropped away. "But now that you've brought up your painting . . ."

She groaned good-naturedly. "I knew it was coming."

"Of course you did. And I've been very good not to bring it up until now, but alas"—he gestured dramatically—"I am capable of being good for only a certain period of time and that time has ended." He looked at her expectantly. "So? When do I get another of your paintings? And is it too much to hope for more than just one?"

She'd already given the matter some thought. "I'll arrange to ship two tomorrow."

An enormous smile wreathed his face. "Excellent! Excellent!" His expression turned calculating. "But as long as you're going to be shipping two, why not consider shipping more? Four perhaps. *Ten*. I could mount a show for you. You know I've been longing to. Say the word and it will be done."

She chuckled. "No show, Winston. Absolutely no show. But very good try, and because you're such a nice man, I'll tell you what I'll do. I'll throw another painting into the shipment."

"*Three*. I'm thrilled!"

"And I think I drank too much wine at lunch," she said dryly.

"Wine?" Jonah said from the open office door behind her. "Now, why didn't I think of that?"

"*Jonah*." Winston immediately surged to his feet. "What a splendid surprise."

"I hope I'm not interrupting." His tone revealed that he spoke out of politeness rather than true concern.

"You're welcome anytime," Winston said. "You know that. Come in. Come in." He gestured to the chair beside Jolie. "Sit down."

Disregarding the chair, Jonah hitched a hip on the corner of the desk so that he was facing her. "Hello, Jolie."

"Hello, Jonah." She'd thought she wouldn't see him again. She'd been working very hard to get herself to accept that fact and to convince herself that it would be all right. But the flush of her skin and the rapid beating of her heart told her her efforts had been wasted. She was incredibly glad to see him again. "Is your meeting finished?"

"We're taking a break, so I called to see if you were here, and when I found out you were, I decided to come over and see how you were."

"I'm fine."

He smiled, reflecting that she gave a new meaning to the word *reticent*. "Did I hear that giving you wine for lunch is a smart move?"

Winston laughed. "It certainly turned out to be a smart move for me. She's just promised me three of her paintings."

"I'll buy all three," Jonah said, his gaze never moving from her face.

Winston's eyes widened.

"No," she said quietly, but firmly.

One dark brow arched. "Why not?"

"Because they're not for you."

"You're putting them up for sale, right? I've got the money to meet whatever price Winston puts on them. What's the problem?"

Because I know you, she thought. Because she put a part of herself in each of her paintings, and selling them was bearable only as long as they went to strangers who wouldn't view their acquisition as a piece of a puzzle that was part of her.

"I'm sure there's no problem," Winston began. "I'm sure we can reach some—"

She stood up. "Thank you for lunch, Winston, but I really do need to start home before the evening rush hour begins." She lightly kissed his cheek.

"You're still going to send me those paintings, aren't you?"

"I'll talk to you soon."

Jonah pushed himself off the desk. "I'll go with you, Jolie." He reached for Winston's hand. "I was serious about buying those paintings. Do not sell them to anyone else."

"Well, no, of course not, but I'm not sure she . . ." Confused, the art dealer watched as the two left his office.

Jolie hurried out of the gallery, not because she thought she could elude Jonah—she knew she couldn't—but because Winston's office seemed to be getting smaller by the minute. Winston and Jonah both wanted something from her, but it was impossible for her to give them everything they wanted. And for a moment in Winston's office, she'd suddenly felt as if she were running out of space and air.

Unfortunately space was at a premium in New York City, and she exited the gallery onto a sidewalk congested with people. Almost immediately she felt Jonah's hand at her elbow, guiding her across the sidewalk, through the crowd, and into the back of a long, black limousine idling at the curb. As easy as that, she was enveloped by quiet, cool air, and the privacy of tinted windows.

"Where are we going?" she asked as the limousine eased away from the curb.

"To Damaron Tower—if that's all right with you."

She sighed. Damaron Tower was a luxurious skyscraper, owned by the Damarons, and made up of offices, apartments, and shops. She had heard that the family occupied the top dozen floors.

"Why?"

"Because I have to go back to the meeting now, but I'll be free in a few hours. I was hoping we could have dinner."

She shook her head. "No." Saying it was the only defense against him she could think of at the moment.

"Not hungry?"

"Not interested."

He gazed at her quietly. "You certainly know how to lay it on the line. What have I done?"

"Nothing." She closed her eyes. "I'm sorry, Jonah. I don't mean to be so abrupt. It's just that I didn't think I'd see you again."

"The last thing I said to you this morning was that I'd see you soon. Did you forget? Or maybe I should ask, did you hope I was wrong?"

She didn't answer him directly. "How much longer do you think your meeting will last?"

"A few hours."

"And what am I supposed to do while you're at the meeting? I have no further business in town."

"There's shopping, museums. You could have the car. I can get you a ticket to any Broadway production you like. Tell me what you'd like to do and I'll arrange it."

Last night she'd agreed to stay in his home in order to get information that would help her break into the house. Her intention had been to use him, and it hadn't worked. She'd gotten nothing of any substance. She hadn't spent her time wisely. She'd allowed herself to become distracted. She'd kissed Jonah and then she'd kissed him again.

And now he was asking her to spend more time with him.

This time she couldn't fool herself. If she accepted his invitation, it would be because she wanted to be with him and no other reason.

That she still had to break into his home to switch the paintings could have no bearing on the matter. Keeping the two activities separate was the only way she would be able to remain sane.

Could she do it? Could she split herself in two like that?

No man had ever commanded her attention the way Jonah had. No man had ever tempted her to divide herself the way she would have to do if she kept seeing him. And she honestly didn't know if she could do it.

"Let *me* put it on the line for you," he said. "I want to see you again. Tonight."

She didn't know if she could do it, she reflected, but she also didn't want to go back home alone with nothing to look forward to but the same argument with her father. And her plans for switching the paintings. Not yet. And she didn't want to leave him. Not yet.

Surely there would be no harm in *trying* to spend a little more time with him, to see if she could truly separate the part of her that was going to deceive him from the part of her that badly wanted to kiss him again.

"Do you have any dogs in your apartment?"

"I told you last night that I don't have any pets. Why?"

"Because I think I'd like to go up to your apartment."

A gleam of satisfaction sparked in his eyes.

SIX

High above the New York City sidewalks, the Damaron cousins were gathered in their large, soundproof board room. Dove-gray suede covered the walls and identical colored blinds slanted a minimal amount of afternoon sunlight into the room.

Jonah stood at the head of the long, polished, onyx conference table, with his cousins ranging around it, sitting in thickly padded chairs upholstered in black glove leather. By design and intent there was no one in the room without the Damaron silver streak.

He was a member of one of the most select clubs in the world: his family. They understood one another as no one else did.

Only he and his cousins ran their family's global business empire. Only he and his cousins were allowed to attend the quarterly business meetings. If for some unavoidable reason one cousin missed a meeting, another would be dispatched to fully brief the absent one. They all shared equally in the responsibilities, the rewards, and the failures.

"Vergara is in prison in Hong Kong," Jonah said, finishing his report, "and his trial date is pending."

A round of applause broke out around the table. Each person had waited a long time to hear the news, which had been placed last on the agenda—their dessert.

"Great work," Lion said solemnly. Like Jonah, Lion was a big man, but his coloring, as befitted his name, was a tawny gold. "There are countries all over the world tonight sighing with relief, thanks to you. Vergara was the world's most wanted terrorist. Interpol will probably give you a medal."

Joanna, her hand resting protectively on her stomach, spoke up. "We are all so grateful, Jonah. There's not one of us who has felt true peace since our parents' plane went down fifteen years ago, knowing that the person who planted the bomb on the plane was walking free. It makes me feel so much better that at least that one particular monster won't be walking free when my baby comes into the world."

Jonah's mouth compressed into a grim line. "There is call for celebration, but a *cautious* celebration. Finding Vergara and bringing him in was a big, big step. But we can't forget that there's another person out there we have yet to bring down, the person who *paid* Vergara to plant that bomb. The person who hated our parents enough to want them dead."

"And that's where I come in," Sin said, looking around the table. "Jonah's done the dirtiest and the hardest part of all of this. Now he needs to rest."

Jonah grinned. "I must really look like hell. That's all I've been hearing since I've been home." Practically in unison, everyone nodded. He laughed. "Thanks, guys."

Sin fixed him with his jade-green eyes. "So you're not going to give us any trouble on this? You're going to take some time off?"

"Normally I would argue with you. I don't like to drop things before they're completely finished, but . . ."

"But this time you will," Sin said, finishing his sentence.

"Yes." Even if he wasn't exhausted and burned out, he'd be very reluctant to leave home now. Because there was Jolie . . .

Jonah took his seat and waved for Sin to take over.

Sin stood. "Tomorrow I'm flying to Hong Kong. Vergara is a stone-cold killer, but everyone has an Achilles' heel, and with the help of Yasmine's computer wizardry"—he nodded in the direction of the lovely young woman with a long, thick topaz plait down her back, a silver streak in her hair, and exotic topaz eyes—"Jonah discovered that Vergara has *two* Achilles' heels—his five-year-old twin sons. There are only a handful of people in the world who know about the twins. Now *we* know, and the information is going to be invaluable to us. Vergara understands that now that he's been captured, there are countries standing in line to prosecute him. If he's not executed by one of those countries, he's going to be in prison for the rest of his life. His options are zero."

Lion nodded. "So he's going to be concerned about the future of his children."

"And that means money," Wyatt Damaron said, anticipating what Sin would say. His silver streak showed prominently against his slightly darker silver-gray hair.

Sin's grin was predatory. "Good old American dollars. We're betting that for enough money, he'll tell us who hired him."

Two one-carat diamonds glinted on the third finger of Joanna's left hand as she asked, "But can we trust the information he gives us?"

"I believe so. This is where our knowledge of his sons is going to come in, because he's going to want more than our money. He's going to want our assurances that we'll keep quiet about his sons. He won't be in any position to

double-cross us by being dishonest, because if
he does, he's taking the chance we'll tell what
we know. But for our insurance, I'm going to
ask for proof of who hired him."

Lion shook his head doubtfully. "That was
fifteen years ago."

"Vergara is a wily predator. He's survived
in the most dangerous world there is for a
long, long time. My guess is he'll have something we can use. But if he doesn't, a name will
still help us. We've had our suspicions for a
long time. All we need is confirmation. Without proof, we may not be able to get our enemy to justice, but we're perfectly capable of
meting out our own brand of punishment."

Sin's gaze went around the room, meeting
the eyes of each of his cousins, and their mur-
mur of agreement was unanimous.

Jonah slowly smiled.

Jolie awoke to find herself lying in Jonah's
huge bed on top of a gold-and-ivory comforter. As she lay there she recalled how he had
brought her to his apartment and shown her
around. When he had left for his meeting, she
had gone into his bedroom, shed her jacket,
curled up on the comforter, and fallen asleep.

She hadn't been particularly tired when she
had decided to take the nap. But she *had* felt
the distinct need to conserve her resources.

She didn't need to be a fortune-teller to know that the next two weeks were going to tax her strength in every way.

She had so much to do. In fact, under the circumstances, accepting Jonah's invitation for dinner had been insane. But given the chance to change her mind, she realized she would make the same decision again.

She was playing with fire, of course. If he ever found out . . . But no, she wouldn't allow that to happen. Besides, this evening's dinner could very well be the last time she saw him.

Years ago, she had reasoned out, then decided, that by avoiding relationships, she could avoid the complications that necessarily arose when secrecy and lies were involved. She'd been successful.

Until Jonah. She hadn't been able to avoid him. Yet she had been forewarned. She remembered feeling uneasy as she had studied his photograph in the paper. Even so, nothing could have prepared her for the dynamic force of Jonah in person. And nothing could have prepared her for the knowledge that she now missed him and couldn't wait for him to come back from his meeting.

As the sun was setting she slid off the bed and set out to explore his apartment. And with each room she passed through, she was reminded of him.

He had chosen most of the things himself, she guessed, unlike his home in the country, which had seemed essentially unchanged for many years. Everywhere she looked, there were strong, sensual lines and colors, and art that appeared to have been collected from all over the world.

She saw a humidor filled with cigars and a large, oval bowl filled with cuff links. In his bathroom she opened the tops of the bottles of cologne and inhaled dark, compelling scents that smelled like Jonah. And she had to wonder—as strange a thought as it was—which had come first, the fragrance or Jonah.

In his closets, she found row after row of shirts, suits, slacks, and sweaters, leather and fine wools, cotton and tweed, all laundered and cleaned, waiting for him. A longing swept over her. It made her wish she'd kept the old shirt of his she'd slept in, so that in months to come she could wrap herself in it and remember. . . .

Lord, she was in trouble.

In his den she fumbled with the stereo until she got it turned on, then chose several CDs to play that featured soothing instrumentals. Settling onto the many-cushioned couch, she watched through the floor-to-ceiling windows as night fell over New York City. And she waited.

◈————————◈

Jonah found her there when he returned. And he was surprised by the deep jolt of satisfaction he felt when he walked in and saw her.

He was used to empty apartments, homes, hotel rooms. It had been his life for a long time. And he had learned to enjoy the quiet and the security of being alone, of not having to watch his back. But tonight he was inexpressibly glad to see Jolie waiting for him.

She looked beautiful, sitting in a pool of gentle lamplight, the gleaming skyline of the city framing her body. There was a softness about her that made his arms ache to hold her. And he would. Soon.

She wasn't easy to know, but he found her interesting as hell. Because of the years he'd spent tracking Vergara, he didn't allow himself to trust easily, which was why he'd been surprised when he realized how quickly, almost without thought, he had come to trust her.

She wasn't as calm or as together as she seemed. There was a turmoil inside her, an edginess that occasionally seeped out. She was wary and cautious, and if ever a woman had secrets, she did. But a normal woman would have bored him. Jolie definitely did not bore him.

He closed the set of double doors behind

him and strolled toward her. "You look rested."

"You don't." His weariness was of the soul as well as the body, she realized for the first time. And the shadows were as prominent as before. "Was your meeting that tough?"

"Tough?" He sat down beside her. "No, not at all." Slowly he reached out, lifted several strands of her silky hair, and let them sift through his fingers. "No," he said again, his voice lower. "Tough is wanting to kiss you as badly as I want to right now and *not* doing it."

She froze, but inside, her blood was heating, thickening. She must have made a soft sound, perhaps of surprise, perhaps of need, because his gaze dropped to her lips. Even her breasts felt as if they were swelling in anticipation of his touch. She had no desire to move away from him. Once again she was waiting for him.

He lowered his head and covered her mouth with his. She made him hungry—hungry to have her, to possess her, to sink into her, to absorb her into him. Right now it was the thing uppermost in his mind. She was all sweet smells, satin skin, and luscious curves, and he wanted her—as easy and as difficult as that was. He slipped his arms around her and brought her against him, deepening and hardening the kiss. His tongue scraped against hers, creating heat and desire, need and aching.

She made another sound that entered his mouth and became a part of him. Just like her taste. Just like her scent.

The life he'd led had dictated that he keep what he felt to himself. Control was all-important, and to lose control could mean disaster. It was a lesson he had learned well.

But with Jolie he found himself struggling for control. He couldn't stop himself from taking more, and she responded like a dream he had never even dared to have.

He had too much experience not to know that she wanted him. But she didn't want him enough yet, not as much as he wanted her to. Even though they were only kissing, he sensed that she was holding back.

But then she did *that*. It was part of what made her an enigma, and it made him all the more determined. He was going to unravel her, mystery by mystery.

In the meantime frustration ate at him because he wanted her closer. Because they both had too many clothes on. Because he needed her naked and beneath him. But for the moment it didn't matter what he wanted or needed. He had to take it one careful step at a time.

He gripped her arms and gently pulled until she slid toward him. Then she arched against him until he felt her nipples through the fabric of their clothes, and a primitive desire to possess her surged through him, to consume, to control.

There was a knock at the double doors. "In the nick of time," he muttered, and inhaled a shaky breath.

Unconsciously she swept her tongue over her bottom lip and tasted him. "What—what was that knock?"

"Our dinner is ready."

"Dinner?" She'd forgotten all about food.

He passed a hand over her hair. "I would have been inconsolable if you hadn't been here waiting for me when I got back from the meeting."

"You don't strike me as the inconsolable type," she said, her voice low and still uneven.

"No?" He pulled farther away so that he could see her better. "Then what type do I strike you as?"

Her inhibitions were disappearing. She could still feel the heat from his kisses. She said what she thought. "Hard. Cold. Intense. And with the ability to be cruel at times."

He furrowed his brow with genuine curiosity. "What have I done to you to make you think I would be cruel or hard or any of those other things?"

"Nothing. Yet."

He studied her thoughtfully. "But you're expecting me to?"

She wished for the words back, but with

Jonah nothing could be taken back, whether it was a smile, or words, or a kiss. "No, because there will be no reason for you to, not to me." She wouldn't be around.

He slid his hand along her jawline and tilted her face up to him. "Tell me, Jolie. Are you always so defensive?"

"I don't think I've ever had to be before."

He stared at her, wondering at the secrets she kept and the mysteries that were a part of her, remembering how good she had felt in his arms, even now feeling how much he still wanted her. "There are some things you should know, Jolie. These past few years I've led a life that's been on the dark side. You name it, I've done it. Often and with great zeal. I've fought, lied, stolen, connived, and that's just the surface."

She wasn't in the least surprised. And somehow she knew he'd been very good at what he'd done. At times his face had a ruthless cast to it that revealed what a tough, merciless man he could be. "And everything you did was very hard on you."

He smiled slightly. "Actually it was incredibly easy."

"Then why the shadows?" She brushed her fingers over the dark circles under his eyes.

His smile increased, and even though it was the most world-weary, cynical smile she had ever seen, she found it incredibly attractive.

"Hard living," he said. "Lack of sleep. Irregular meals. All of it and more. I'm used to doing anything I have to do to get what I want."

"I knew that before you told me."

"How?"

"I looked into your eyes."

It was an incredible thing for her to say and he had to pause to absorb her words. "Good," he finally said, "then you're warned."

"I was warned the minute I looked at you."

The knock came at the door again. "Apparently we have a chef who doesn't like his meal to grow cold. I think our dinner is ready." His hand encircled her arm as he surged to his feet and brought her with him. "Come on, I'll tell you a little of what I've been doing while we eat."

He tugged her forward, but she held back. "Why will you tell me only a little?"

"Because if you knew everything I've done, I might never see you again."

She also had secrets, she thought as she followed him, secrets that she would never tell him for the very same reason. It didn't matter what he'd done; he wouldn't want to have anything to do with her if he knew she was a thief. He wouldn't want to see her if he knew she planned to circumvent *his* security system and break into *his* house. And despite everything, she wanted him to want to continue seeing her. The knowledge rocked her to her toes.

Their dinner was served in a stone-and-crystal dining room. A rough stone pedestal supported a glass-topped table. Candlesticks chipped out of stone held candles that reached halfway to the ceiling. Their flames glinted in the heavy crystal glasses and vied with the lights blazing beyond the window.

Jonah sat her to his right, close enough that he could reach out and touch her if he wished, lean over and inhale her feminine scent if he chose, lean over and kiss her if he desired. But for now he was content to have her next to him, content enough to tell her a little of what he'd gone through during the past years.

"Fifteen years ago my cousins and I all became orphans at the same time. My parents and my aunts and uncles were killed one sunny day when they were all flying together to Switzerland, and their plane went down in the Alps."

She laid down her fork. "Jonah, how terrible for all of you. I can't even imagine how traumatic it must have been for you and your cousins."

He nodded. "It was like the end of our world. We were very young, but we aged overnight."

"I can see how you would."

"We inherited everything—the businesses,

the properties, the money, and the responsibilities. We had no choice but to grow up fast.
We had advisers, but they were in it for what
they could earn. We were in it for us, for our
family. So we quickly learned to circle the wag-
ons and rely only on one another."

A little of Jonah's personal history went a
long way to explaining that ruthless cast in his
face, she thought. But knowing how he had
become who he was today didn't change who
he was. Still, just for a moment she allowed
herself to wonder if he could ever soften, perhaps settle down. Then she quickly dismissed
the thought as foolishness on her part. "I don't
follow business news, but a person would have
to spend a lot of time on Mars not to know
that your family has had some extraordinary
successes in business."

"Yes, we have. And now we've done something else."

"Oh? What?"

"When that plane went down, we were just
kids. But after the one funeral that was for all
of our parents, we gathered at Sin's house. And
we agreed that if we did nothing else, we
would find the person or persons responsible
for our parents' death, and one way or another
we would bring them to justice."

At that moment he looked harder than she
had ever seen him look before. "One way or
another?"

"We always try the law first, but if that doesn't work, we resort to our own brand of justice."

He said it as if it was the most reasonable thing on earth. She felt a chill shiver over her, a chill of fear. People who wronged him or his family didn't stand a chance. And knowing that, she still had to go through with her plan. "You were young then. It would be understandable if, over time, living became more important to you all than getting revenge for the dead."

"We've never backed down one inch from that agreement."

She studied him. "And *you* took on the lion's share of the work."

He had not told her that, and yet she understood, he thought. What else would she understand? "Have you heard of the terrorist Vergara?"

Her eyes widened. "Of course." Worldwide intelligence organizations had been searching for the man for over twenty years. Countless deaths and untold suffering had been traced directly to him.

"He's the one who planted the bomb on the plane. It took us a long time to trace it to him, but we finally did. We all worked on it, but I was the one who did most of the actual tracking."

"But I've heard that no one can find him. I

once read that Interpol has a special unit dedicated to him."

"Their unit can quit looking."

She could only imagine the kind of relentlessness it had taken to run to ground someone like Vergara. She felt the chill again. "Is he alive?" Somehow the question was important to her. She needed to know whether he'd killed Vergara or not. She believed he was capable. She believed he had every reason. But had he?

"Alive and living in a Hong Kong prison cell."

She was glad. He was dealing with enough without having to deal with blood on his hands, no matter how good the reason. "But I haven't heard anything about his capture."

"The authorities are trying to keep the news under wraps for as long as they can. They want this time to interrogate him without having to deal with the media. They have quite a few incidents they want to question him about." He grimaced. "If he'll cooperate."

"And you captured him." It was such an amazing feat that she had to repeat it.

"It took me years, but yes, I did."

There was such a power about Jonah, such a life force. As amazing as it was, she believed him implicitly when he told her he'd captured Vergara. In fact, she wouldn't doubt it if he told her he had set the world spinning in the opposite direction.

He reached for her hand, taking it in his. "You're looking very apprehensive, Jolie. What's wrong?"

"I was just thinking that it would be a very bad idea to cross you."

"You're not planning on it, are you?" he asked in a light tone that told her it would never occur to him that she would do so.

But she was planning on it and he could never know. She'd never forget this night, sitting high in the sky at a glistening glass table, with him holding her hand. She felt as if he had her wrapped up in his energy and vitality. He was a fascinating man, a man whose like she would never meet again. He affected her, he moved her, he made her catch fire, but he wasn't meant for her. She had things she had to do, and afterward she would get back to her own life.

She wasn't hungry, but she picked up her fork and began to eat.

He watched her for a minute, then followed suit. "Do you like the food?"

"It's very good. Where did it come from? I took a tour of the apartment when I woke up, but I didn't see anyone else. You mentioned a chef?"

"Since I'm rarely here, I don't have a full-time cook, but there's a corporate chef for our offices here and I had him prepare this meal."

"It's wonderful."

"I'm glad you like it." He continued to look at her, and for a moment she knew what it was like to be hypnotized. It wasn't that he was actively trying to make her fall under his spell. No. Everything he did came naturally to him, which made everything he did that much more effective. How many scores of women all over the world had fallen under his spell? she wondered. And how had they put their hearts back together after he left them?

"Thank you for staying in town this evening," he murmured.

"What would you have done if I hadn't? Would you have gone back to your house in the country? Or would you have stayed here and had dinner with your cousins?"

Curiosity had made her ask the question. She could envision lonely nights ahead when she'd wonder where he was and what he was doing. And she would also wonder a great deal about whom he was with.

She pushed away her plate. It was nearly impossible to eat sitting this close to him. A heated tension pervaded the atmosphere. She felt it over her entire body. She couldn't do two things at once, and in the end there was no contest. Jonah required her full attention.

"What would I have done?" he asked, his

eyes unreadable as he looked at her. "I would have missed you like hell. Are you through eating?"

"Yes."

He tossed his napkin onto the table. "Go back into the den. I'll bring us coffee and brandy."

"No brandy for me." She rarely drank. She needed a steady hand and a clear head for her art, for protecting her father, and now for protecting herself against Jonah.

"Then I'll bring you coffee."

In the den she tried to calm her nerves. Perhaps a brandy wouldn't be entirely amiss after all, she reflected wryly. It might ease the tightness in her stomach, ease the knots that seemed to tie and retie themselves every time she looked at Jonah.

Leaning back against the pillows of the couch, she gazed around the den, trying to relax. Even though its contents alone were probably worth ten times the value of her whole house, it was a comfortable room. Yet he said he was rarely here. She wondered if that was going to change now that Vergara was in jail.

Lord, she wished she could stop trying to figure out what he would be doing once she left his life. Being able to picture him here or in his home in the country wouldn't make her being alone again any easier.

She looked up as he entered the room, carrying a tray with coffee and brandy. "I was just wondering if you would be using this apartment and your house more often now that you have accomplished your goal of capturing Vergara. They're both so wonderful. It's a shame to leave them empty so much of the time."

He sat down beside her and poured her coffee. "I'm glad you like them. I have a couple of other places too. But to answer your question, yes, I plan to stay here for a while."

"Here? In the city?"

He handed her a cup. "Yes and the house in the country too. But I'll probably be here for the next week."

She hadn't asked him about his plans in order to get useful information from him, she reflected, sipping at the coffee, but his answer was nonetheless valuable to her. If she hurried, she could have the paintings switched before he returned to the country.

He poured himself a brandy and sat back beside her. "You want to hear something that I think is interesting?"

"Certainly."

"I know nothing about you."

She hadn't seen that one coming. If she had guessed the subject of conversation was about to turn to her, she wouldn't have been so quick to show interest. "Yes, of course, you do."

He held up a finger. "Ah, you see, that's the really interesting part. You have a way of *making* me feel that I do, but then when I look back on our conversations, I realize they've all been about me. You willingly give nothing up about yourself. You give me the verbal equivalent of smoke and mirrors, and I'm curious as to why."

She sat the cup and saucer down. "You're mistaken. If I don't talk about myself, it's because there's nothing of any real interest to say. I don't travel around the world. I stay home, live with my father, and paint. All of which you know. You even know my father. You've employed him."

"And that's *all* I know. Superficial facts. And when I indicated I wanted to purchase your three paintings, you said no. Why?"

She didn't have a good answer for him, so she said the first thing that came to her. "They wouldn't go with your decor."

"Sorry, but I don't buy it. When you said no, you didn't have a clue what my apartment is like."

"I knew what your home in the country looks like. Monets, Renoirs, and van Goghs are hanging in your home." She forced a quick smile. "Trust me. My paintings wouldn't fit in."

"I trust you," he said slowly. "And I still know nothing about you. Once again you've told me nothing."

She shrugged uneasily. "I'll tell you anything you want to know."

"Right. Sure you will. And I'll bet you'll even let me check up your sleeve. The problem is, there won't be anything there, will there?"

"May I have a small amount of brandy, please?"

"You can have anything you want, Jolie." He poured her a glass of brandy and handed it to her, then leaned back and looked at her again. "What is it you want?"

She wanted one night all alone in his country house with the security system off, she thought. *That's* what she wanted. And she wanted him never to find out what she'd done. And as long as she was wishing, she'd like for him always to look at her as he was looking at her tonight—as if she was endlessly fascinating and utterly desirable.

But she couldn't have any of those things.

She took a swallow of the brandy and briefly closed her eyes while its heat curled its way through her. It felt good, bracing.

"Jolie," she heard him say. "Tell me what you want."

She opened her eyes. "Peace and love for all mankind."

His lips quirked. "Sounds like a Christmas card."

"Sounds perfect to me."

"And it sounds to me as if once again you're evading my question."

She took another swallow of the brandy. It was doing a beautiful job of untying the knots in her stomach. Unfortunately Jonah had a way of creating new knots, new tensions. "I'm not evading your question."

"When I first met you, I had the feeling you didn't like being the center of attention, that if you'd had your wish, you would have simply faded into the woodwork. But you're not shy."

"No. I'm simply not much of a party person. I was there for my father."

"He must be very proud of you."

"Proud of me?" She'd have liked to think so, but who knew? Her father was off in his own world, most of the time barely aware of what she was doing. But she wouldn't be human if she didn't wish that he were proud of her.

"According to Winston Blakely, you are an extremely talented artist." He reached out and touched her throat where color was slowly creeping upward. His fingers lightly stroked the color, then settled at the base of her neck where her pulse beat rapidly. "You're getting agitated, aren't you? You really don't handle it well when the talk turns to you. Why?"

Heat was gathering where his fingers were touching her, but she couldn't lose her concentration now. She had to find an answer to give him, an answer that would satisfy. "I work long hours by myself. Days go by when the only other person I see is my father and then for only a few minutes out of the day. I'm used to being alone."

"Sounds boring."

"I couldn't work with people around me. Maybe that's the reason I'm not comfortable with attention."

He shook his head in confused amazement. "How can that be? You're *beautiful*. I can't be the first man who's ever told you that."

He thought she was beautiful. The knowledge had the same effect on her as consuming an entire bottle of brandy. A dizziness swept over her. "No."

His mouth quirked. "There's a certain part of me that wishes I were. Tell me about these men who have told you you're beautiful."

"I don't want to talk about them any more than you probably would want to tell me about the women who've been in your life."

"If you wanted me to tell you, I'd try, but the thing is, I can't remember any one before you."

"That's a very convenient memory lapse."

"But true. The only woman in my mind right now is you."

She believed him. He was concentrating on her with such intensity; her skin felt scorched.

She drew in a deep breath. "You know what? I need to go home." She looked around for a phone. "I should order a car." Of course she'd have to send Winston another painting to pay for the car, she thought ruefully. "No, on second thought I'll just take the train."

"I'll fly you home. You'll save two hours. And that's two extra hours you can be here with me. And since I don't seem to be having a great deal of luck figuring out the puzzle of you, I think I'll do something else."

While she was trying to sort through what he'd said, he slid his hand to the back of her neck, brought her toward him, and took her mouth in an electrifying kiss.

Caught unaware, she made a soft sound of surprise that quickly quieted as tempestuous feelings rushed over her. And suddenly she realized that this kiss was exactly what she'd been wanting all evening long. She'd thought it was enough simply to be with him, to watch his mouth move when he smiled and spoke, to watch his eyes glitter when he looked at her, to watch his big hands and his long fingers move as he gestured.

But now she realized that she was tired of trying to monitor what she said, tired of worrying about the nearly impossible job ahead of her of replacing the paintings, tired of worrying about her father.

She wanted to feel Jonah's hands exploring

her body and his mouth tasting her skin. And most shocking of all, she wanted to watch his face as he climaxed inside her.

No, she quickly corrected herself. She *couldn't* want that. To make love to him would be a commitment she couldn't afford. Kissing him would have to be enough. Having him hold and touch her would have to satisfy.

And afterward . . . she didn't know. And she couldn't think about it right now.

He gathered her against him, and with a sigh of happiness she went.

He paused at the sound, but then her mouth opened wider beneath his and he couldn't resist. His tongue thrust deeper, taking what she was offering. He could taste the brandy and coffee. He could taste her sweetness and he could feel her heat. And he was overwhelmed by it all, by her.

She presented him with a challenge that no other woman ever had. He couldn't seem to break her particular code, the code that would tell him what made her tick, what made her laugh, what made her cry. With most women, he wouldn't have cared. But with Jolie he did. Passionately.

He wouldn't rest until he had learned everything there was to know about her. But for now, he was going to learn her body, learn what made her breathe quickly, what made her cry out, what made her beg for more. He was going to learn well. And then he was going to make her his.

Slowly he leaned back into the corner of the couch, bringing her with him so that she was half lying on top of him, pliant and willing, her curves fitting into him seamlessly. Kissing her was like drinking clear, cool water on a hot day. He couldn't get enough and he couldn't stop. The act of kissing her was necessary, compulsive, addictive. "I don't know who taught you to kiss," he muttered against her mouth, "but I want to either thank him or kill him."

How could she tell him that kissing him seemed the most natural thing in the world to her when she didn't understand it herself? Every flick and thrust of her tongue, every movement of her mouth was instinctive. She didn't think about it. She simply did it. And for now she was going to enjoy it.

He stretched his long legs out along the sofa and shifted her so that she was lying completely on top of him, her pelvis nestled over his. He hadn't intended to go even this far, but she was too tempting.

He worked her T-shirt upward until he reached her lace bra, a bit of nothing that didn't stop him. He slid his hand beneath the bra and took hold of one firm breast. She filled his big hand and he could feel her nipple, a tight hard bead, pressing into his palm. She arched against him, and with a groan, he took the nipple between his finger and thumb and lightly tugged, then toyed with it until she was squirming against him, whimpering with pleasure.

He was experienced with women. He'd been the object of countless seductions. He'd seduced countless women. But Jolie overwhelmed him. He wanted her so badly, he was shaking. He was swollen, aching. He thrust his hips up to her, the motions that of the age-old act of sex.

Sharp pleasure stabbed through her, quick and urgent, as she felt his hard arousal push against her. Instinctively she spread her legs slightly so that his erection would press at the juncture of her thighs, the spot where heat had pooled, pleasure, pain.

And when she did, he tensed, fearful he would lose his control, right then and there. He was burning for her. He was dying for her. He wanted to be tender with her, take all the time in the world. He wanted to rip her clothes off, take her hard and fast. "How can I want you so much?" he asked hoarsely.

She was wrestling with the same thing. She knew what she wanted now. Against all reason, against all caution and logic, she wanted to make love with him.

Her fingers went to his shirt and attacked the long line of buttons. He helped and soon

his shirt was open and her nipples were nest-
ling in the dark curling hair that covered his
chest. And still she hurt, ached, needed more.
There was a fire in her belly, a fire in her soul,
and she desperately wanted to go with the feeling, to let loose, to enjoy fully.

His hand slipped between them, and with
deft fingers he undid the waistband of her
slacks, then slid the flat of his palm down over
her stomach, heading to the area between her
legs, the most sensitive, secret place on her
body. He was about to show her a heaven she
hadn't known existed, and who could resist
heaven?

She knew the answer, even if she hated it.
She had no choice but to try.

Stiffening, she pulled slightly away so that
his hand stilled on her stomach.

"Jolie?" he murmured. "You can trust me."

She believed him. No matter what he had
done in the past or what he was capable of
doing in the future, she did know that she
could trust him. He was the type of man to
stand beside in a time of troubles. She also
sensed he would be the type of man who would
take great care of her while he made love to
her, protecting her, pleasuring her.

But there was one problem that he didn't
know about. *He couldn't trust her.* And the guilt
was too much for her.

Embarrassed beyond belief, she shifted off

him and struggled to her feet, straightening her clothes as she went.

He bolted upright on the couch. "Jolie, what's wrong?"

"Nothing." She wrapped her arms around herself. "I just can't do this. I'm sorry."

He surged to his feet and closed the distance between them, concern written in his features. "Why not? What did I do? Tell me."

She backed away. "You did nothing wrong. It's just . . . I've got to go."

His fists opened and closed as he stood in the middle of the room and gazed bleakly at her, but he didn't follow her. "I've frightened you." His tone was flat, with an edge of disappointment. "I pushed you too far too fast. I told you too much."

"What?" With her senses still spinning, she wasn't certain what he meant.

"I shouldn't have told you about Vergara."

"Vergara? No, Jonah." She started to go to him, to put her hand on his arm, to reassure him. But she was afraid that if she touched him again, she wouldn't be able to let go, not soon, not easily. "You're wrong. Nothing you told me frightened me. Vergara is evil and now he's out of commission. As far as I'm concerned the end justifies the means."

"Then what is it?"

She tried to remember what he'd said, then

grabbed at a straw. "Too fast—it's been too fast."

His gaze was brooding as he folded his arms across his chest. His hands, she noted, were still clenched into fists.

"That didn't seem to be a problem a few minutes ago. The way you were responding—"

She rushed to cut him off before he could remind her of how she'd acted. "You said it yourself. You don't know me."

"But what I know I like, so much so in fact, I can't get you out of my mind. Jolie, don't you trust me?"

Trust—there was that word again. "Yes, yes, I do."

"Then come back to the couch. We won't do anything you don't want to. And no matter what, I'll stop when you say to. I didn't give you an argument a few minutes ago, did I? Or if you'd rather, we'll simply talk."

She couldn't remember ever feeling so miserable or so helpless. Ironically she wasn't used to deceit on a one-on-one basis. What she did, stealing into people's homes without their knowledge, switching works of art, didn't involve face-to-face interaction with anyone. Which was good. She was terrible at lying through her teeth.

On the other hand, it was plain he wasn't used to having to talk a woman into staying with him, although he was very good at what he was trying to do. But no matter how badly she might want to do as he wanted, she couldn't. "Look"—she spread her hands out placatingly—"I'm sorry. I can't apologize enough, but I have some things I have to work out."

"Like what?"

"Personal things." She shook her head, refusing to say more. "I've got to go, Jonah."

He threw up his hands. "Fine, if that's what you want." He walked to the phone. "I'll order the chopper."

"No, I prefer to go home on my own." She needed to get away from him.

He picked up the phone and punched in some numbers. "All right, Jolie, but you're not taking the train. I'm ordering a car."

She decided not to argue. Under the circumstances, he was being very nice, but she could see the frustration seething just beneath his surface. And she didn't blame him. He obviously wasn't used to having a woman walk out on him without him knowing the reason why.

He hung up the phone with a control that told her he would have preferred to slam it down. "By the time you get downstairs, the car will be there."

"Thank you."

He nodded, his expression more somber than she had ever seen it. "Jolie, I know how important trust is. I've spent the past few years in situations where I could trust no one. But you can trust me. And believe me, that's something I've never told a woman before."

She was tempted to go back to him and damn the consequences. But there was her father to consider, her father who had always been strong for her, and now that their roles were reversed, she had to be strong for him.

If she could convince him to stop the forgeries, and *if* she could successfully return the last of the paintings so that Jonah would never know what had happened, then perhaps she and Jonah would have a chance. "I'm going to be busy for the next two weeks."

"Two weeks is a long time, Jolie. What's so damned important?"

"It's something I have to do for my father. But after that, maybe . . . if you're still interested, we could see each other again."

"I assure you, Jolie. Still being interested in you won't be a problem."

SEVEN

"Papa, would you like tea with dinner?" Jolie held out a pitcher of iced tea. "Papa?" He didn't answer. "Papa?" She walked over to the kitchen table where he was sitting and thrust the pitcher beneath his nose. "Tea?"

His head jerked up. "What's that?"

"It's tea, Papa. Do you want a glass to go with your dinner?"

"That would be nice."

She returned to the counter, poured his glass, then placed it directly in front of him. The last couple of days he had been more preoccupied with his own thoughts than usual. There were times when she found his absent-mindedness endearing. This evening wasn't one of them. She'd spent the last few days studying Jonah's security system, and tonight was the night she planned to get through it.

Up until this moment she hadn't given her father's absentmindedness much thought. But now that she really took the time to look at him, she realized she didn't like what she was seeing.

Forgetting dinner for a moment, she drew a chair next to him and sat down. "Papa, what's wrong?" Gently she put her hand on his cheek and turned his face to her. "Papa?"

His eyes slowly focused on her. "Jolie Christiane."

"You don't look well." She pressed the back of her hand to his forehead, but his skin was cool. "What is it?"

"Jolie Christiane." Sadness etched his lined face as he held his hand straight out. "I felt my hand shake today."

"Oh, Papa, I'm so sorry." She knew it had been hard for him to have to confront his own mortality like that. "But now do you believe me when I tell you that you can't continue with the forgeries?"

His jaw set. "I cannot give up my work. I would have nothing else to do."

She put her hand on his arm and squeezed reassuringly. "Your real work is the restoration, and you can still do most of it. There is no one better than you, Papa. You can give new life to a damaged painting. That's a gift and you can still do it."

"Restoration?" He looked at her as if he had just heard the word for the first time.

She bit back her impatience. "You can still restore the art. You just cannot—Papa, you *must* not—forge anymore. You will be caught."

"Perhaps for a little while longer—"

"*No!* Not one day longer. What you have been doing is a crime."

Clearly agitated, he ran his hand through his disorderly white hair. "No one has been hurt."

Her nerves were too on edge to engage in another futile argument with him. The job before her tonight was monumental, and it was going to take steady nerves, plus all her concentration.

With a sigh she changed tactics. "Tomorrow I'm going to make you a doctor's appointment. I want you to have a thorough checkup." The fact that his hands were shaking could simply be a sign of advancing age, but it also could indicate something more serious.

She had expected him to object vehemently, but to her surprise he lapsed back into his own private thoughts, his expression dejected and depressed.

She hadn't gotten him to agree to stop forging works of art, but he had admitted that he did have a problem. It was a start, she thought, clinging to hope.

❖━━━━━❖

It was now or never, Jolie thought, gazing at the back of Jonah's house. She just wished she felt more prepared, but she never began a job full of confidence. For one thing, she hated what she had to do. She received no thrill from her feats. For another, confidence bred mistakes. In her experience, it wasn't the big things that tripped a person up, it was the little ones.

But tonight the conditions couldn't have been more perfect. No dogs. Jonah was gone. A mild night with only a sliver of a moon that frequently disappeared behind clouds.

From her vantage point approximately fifty yards from the house, she could see only a few inside lights on. The grounds weren't lit. Big mistake, Jonah, she told him silently. If it were her home and those were her paintings hanging in the salon, she would have every inch of the yard lit. But then, it wasn't her home.

She hugged the perimeter of the main yard with its rows of shrubs. She advanced carefully, without hurry.

Jonah had the most sophisticated system she had ever encountered, and to get in and get out without being detected was going to take every bit of skill she had accumulated over the past years. The system had every bell and whistle she had ever heard about and some she hadn't encountered until she had begun to study this one.

If things went well, she would have a couple of hours inside the house to work. Not that she would need that much time.

She paused in the shadow of a tree. She could smell the faint scent of chlorine from the nearby swimming pool. In contrast, the fragrance of roses and gardenias was surprisingly potent. And somewhere smoke drifted on the air. The gardener had probably burned leaves during the day.

Strapped to her back in a special harness she had devised were the two Matisse paintings and the Renoir, along with a small backpack of necessary tools. It would only be a matter of taking the fakes out of the frames and replacing them with the originals. Ten minutes tops for all three of them.

As a precaution she had called the house that day about noon, and spoke to Reynolds, using a made-up name. He had confirmed that Jonah was not in residence. Unless the alarms sounded, the staff would stay in their quarters. Consequently she felt confident that once inside the house, she wouldn't be interrupted.

Staring up at the rear balcony that curved out from Jonah's bedroom, she wondered what he was doing tonight. These last few days she had had to fight to keep her mind on the business at hand. He was embedded in her consciousness and she couldn't get him out. He was a force in her life now and she had no choice but to deal with him. She didn't have a clue what would happen between them once she had accomplished her task and made sure her father was protected. But she did know that she was going to have to find out.

She took a deep breath and caught a stronger whiff of the smoke as she started out again. The sooner this was over, the sooner she could call Jonah. The thought of hearing his voice again sent her heart beating wildly.

Her foot caught on a rake, she lost her balance, and the rake's handle flew sideways and slammed into a terra-cotta pot with a loud *thwack.*

"Who's there?"

The blood froze in her veins. *Jonah.* His voice had come from the second-story balcony. Oh, Lord, he was home.

"Who's there?"

Remembering a break in the hedge a few feet back, she retreated there and stepped into it just as lights flooded the grounds, the lights she had expected to find on in the first place.

She heard no footsteps, but she had no doubt he was coming down the staircase. Her heart was beating out of control now and her hands were shaking, but she forced herself to concentrate on one thing at a time. She quickly stripped out of the harness, then carefully slid the paintings behind a hedge, following the paintings with the backpack.

Then she rapidly sorted through her options. She could stay where she was and try to hide. When he found the rake and the broken pot, he might think a stray animal had done the damage. But there was the chance he might not be satisfied with that explanation and conduct a more thorough search. If he did, he might find her gear and the paintings.

Lifting her hand to shield her eyes against the light, she stepped from behind the hedge and saw him, his tall, imposing figure striding across the lawn toward her.

"Jolie?" he called loudly. "Good God, is that you?"

"Yes, it's me."

She started toward him, her aim to draw him away from the paintings. But also because it seemed inevitable that she did so. He was like a magnet. Even in the middle of the night, when she'd been intent on a crime, she couldn't stop her senses from responding to the sight of him.

Reaching her, he grasped her arms, delighted and puzzled. "What are you doing here? And at this time of night?"

"I—I came to see you."

"Why didn't you call? I would have come and gotten you."

He had caught her in the act of trying to

steal from him, but he must never know. Yet seeing him again so unexpectedly, she was having trouble thinking. She hadn't been prepared to lie and to fight against his overpowering draw at the same time. "Because I didn't know you were going to be here. And I didn't know I was . . . going to be here. I just got in the car and started driving."

"But why did you come here if you thought I wasn't here? And why the back? Why not the front?"

"I was just driving. I—I'm sorry. I shouldn't have trespassed."

He drew her against him, folding his arms around her, enveloping her with his heated masculinity. Then he surprised her by pressing his lips to her temple, for the moment almost reverently.

"Don't be foolish," he whispered huskily. "You have no idea how badly I wanted to see you."

At that moment she had to admit to herself how badly she had wanted to see him.

He pulled away and gazed down at her, then bent his head and covered her mouth with his. She tasted smoke—he'd been smoking, she realized with surprise—and desire. It didn't seem to matter that they had been apart for several days. Their desire for each other was still there, the basic, raw need just beneath the skin. And they only had to see each other for it to race to the surface.

"I was sitting up on the balcony," he said, smoothing the back of his hand along her cheek, "thinking of you, wishing for you, brooding because you weren't with me. And when I saw you, I had this absurd notion that I had conjured you up." He laughed at himself and took her hand. "Come on. I'll show you how beautiful the night is from the balcony."

He was going to accept her explanation, she thought, following him. But then why shouldn't he? He had no reason to think that she would be there for any other reason than to see him. She felt incredible relief and even more guilt.

"When did you get back?" she asked.

"Late this afternoon. I finished what I needed to do early and couldn't think of any good reason to stay there. And I have a full agenda here that requires my attention." He pulled her up the stairs after him to the balcony. "But when I couldn't sleep, I decided to come out, have a cigar, and enjoy the night."

She saw the still-burning cigar resting in an ashtray beside one of the chairs. "I didn't know you smoked." She said it, then remembered seeing the humidor in his apartment.

"I do only occasionally." He bent to stub the cigar out, then drew her along the balcony to a long couch with sailcloth-covered cushions. "Come sit down with me and tell me what you've been doing these last few days."

"I've been working." She should leave as soon as possible, she thought. Everything was going really well—he believed her—but there was no sense in pushing her luck. She was certain he'd insist on walking her to her car. She could drive off and, after about an hour, circle back to get the paintings. Switching the paintings was going to be much trickier since he was in residence. He probably wouldn't fall asleep until very early in the morning, so that narrowed her window of opportunity. She'd simply have to work within that window.

"You've been painting?"

"Yes." Each lie she told him tore at her. She couldn't wait until the Renoir and the Matisse paintings were back safely where they belonged.

"You're wearing black." With a sweep of his hand he indicated her jeans, T-shirt, and tennis shoes. "The first time I saw you, you were wearing black. It looks good on you."

Self-consciously she smoothed her hand down her jeans. "When I set out for my drive, I didn't expect to see anyone. I also didn't expect to be gone long, either, so I can't stay but a few minutes."

"What happened, Jolie?"

"What do you mean?"

"You told me you couldn't see me for two

weeks, that you were going to be busy. Something to do with your father, now that I think about it. Yet you take a drive and show up at my house. What happened?"

"I have been busy and it does have to do with my father. And I didn't know you were going to be here."

"But you did come here."

It was a statement, but she responded as if it were a question. "Yes."

He gave a muffled oath. "You know what? I don't care why you came. Only that you did and that you're here with me now."

He'd said he had been wishing for her, and when she'd tripped on that rake, she had been thinking of him. Earlier she'd smelled the smoke. Perhaps subconsciously she had known that he was here and had wanted him to hear her. Whatever, she knew she was awfully glad to see him again.

He brushed his fingers down the side of her neck, then cupped the nape of her neck with his hand beneath her hair. "I don't care about anything but making love to you."

She could leave. He wouldn't stop her. She should leave. But she didn't want to. And there it was, the *truth*. She wanted to stay, because she realized she, too, cared about nothing more than making love to him.

"Yes," she said, answering the question that hadn't been asked yet.

A shudder swept through him. He'd been sitting all alone in the dark silence, as he had so many times before, and then she had appeared, a longing brought to life.

The edginess was still with her, as was the cloak of mystery she wore as naturally as she wore perfume. Her hair was a silky cloud, her eyes showed fire and doubt. He would eradicate the doubt, he thought, and then he would increase the fire.

It was easy to pull the T-shirt from her waistband, easy to slide his hand up her skin to her breast. Her bra was pushed aside, and then he was holding her in his hand. He breathed her in as he kissed her, taking her taste into him and her smell.

It was a smell and taste he hadn't been able to forget. Four days had seemed like years. There was no way he would have been able to last two weeks. In the city, surrounded by millions of people, he had been alone and had wanted her. In the country, surrounded by no one, he had still wanted her.

He wasn't certain he'd ever be able to let her go again.

He felt a tremor sweep through her as he thumbed her rigid nipple and drove his tongue as deep as he could into her mouth. His body was already hard, ready, and aching. He was going to thrust deep into her and he wasn't sure he was going to stop, even at dawn.

During these past few days when he hadn't been with her, he'd thought of her, of the way she went pliant against his body, of the small sounds she made at the back of her throat when he kissed and touched her. As she was doing now.

Need was building in him. Hard, sharp-edged desire. The unbearable kind that once a man experienced, he could never do without again. She was that need, that desire. Jolie.

He gathered her against him and surged with her to his feet. "We're going into the bedroom," he said.

She wasn't certain of distance or even how she moved. She walked with him, kissed him, clutched at him. Her T-shirt came off over her head and disappeared. Her bra followed, as did more kisses. She gasped but didn't know why.

She heard herself cry out when he lifted her high in the air and sucked her nipple into his mouth. An electrical current sliced through her body, rendering her almost helpless. She wrapped her legs around his waist and held on to him.

There were more kisses and touches, on her mouth, on her nipples and breasts. The fresh night air turned into the breeze from a ceiling fan. Lights from the balcony became the light from a single bedside lamp.

She fell backward and he came with her, and still she held tightly to him. She was breathing hard, as if she'd run a race. Tension gripped her, heat enveloped her, but she felt softer than she had ever felt in her life, as if she were capable of flowing into him and around him and becoming part of him.

"Jolie?"

She opened her eyes and met his gaze. His eyes were smiling, and it was the most seductive sight she had ever seen.

"You trust me," he said as if he had just decided.

"Of course I do."

"Ah, sweet Jolie." The smile disappeared from his eyes, leaving behind intense fire. "You won't be sorry."

Her jeans were tight, but with amazing dexterity he had them undone and skimmed them down and off her legs. His gaze swept the length of her, over the flatness of her stomach, to the black bikini panties, to her long legs, and a groan rumbled up from his chest. "Do you have any idea what you do to me?"

Somehow, sometime, she'd unbuttoned his shirt. His skin was tight and hot, the hair that covered his chest curly, slightly wiry, yet soft. She placed her palm against his heart and felt it pound. "I know what you do to me." She lifted her head slightly and pressed a kiss to his nipple, then let her tongue flick out to taste it.

"It's nothing compared to what I'm about

to do." His voice was a mixture of a growl and a snarl.

Growing frustrated, she pushed at his shirt, finally getting it off his shoulders. He shrugged out of it, but he was clearly more interested in her than in finishing the job of undressing. He smoothed his hand down over her stomach, beneath the edge of the black panties, to the wetness and heat between her legs.

It took only a light touch from him to make her shudder with pleasure. When he did it again, she moaned. "Jonah . . ."

"Yes," he murmured, kissing her stomach. He didn't know where his control was coming from. Inside, he was a furnace. Inside, he was made up of cravings and hungers only she could assuage. Later he would contemplate the power she had over him and decide what to do about it. But for now, everything about her was important to him. He didn't want to overlook any part. He peeled the panties from her, then found again the sweet spot between her legs, the place that made her turn her head back and forth and moan his name. He blew a soft hot breath onto her stomach, then kissed his way up to her breasts.

Her fingers clenched on his shoulders as she felt his fingers move inside her and his mouth fasten onto her breast. She was shaking with need, growing more and more desperate for him. She hadn't known what she expected, but certainly not this power of emotion, not the pleasure that was so forceful it took over completely, obliterating time, place, and reason.

His every kiss was winding her tighter and tighter, his every touch was making her that much wilder. Then suddenly his teeth lightly clamped on one of her nipples, and his finger moved inside her just so, and then she was crying out and arching upward and the world was spinning out of control.

He watched her, savage delight ripping through him as her climax ripped through her. From this night on, she was going to be his and his alone.

When once again she lay still, her heated flesh quivering, he quickly rid himself of his clothes, then came over her, his big body covering her, his pelvis between her thighs. Resting his weight on his elbows, he framed her face with his hands and smoothed her hair off her forehead. "I've been around the world more times than I can count," he murmured, "and I've never seen anything like you."

"You're amazing," she whispered.

With a soft, husky chuckle he positioned himself and eased into her. When he first encountered the barrier, he stopped, not certain what he was feeling.

"It's all right," she whispered, and ran her

hands over his back, feeling the muscles roll and tense.

"You've never . . . ?"

"It's all right," she said again. "Make love to me."

A hard shudder racked his body. Passion had him in its grip, clawing demandingly at him. His mind was having trouble assimilating the meaning of what he now knew to be true.

She clutched at him. "Jonah . . . please, oh, please."

He pulled his hips back and thrust into her. She cried out, and for the first time he heard pain in her voice. As much as it would have cost him, he almost stopped, but then he felt her move beneath him, arching and rotating her hips, and he couldn't hold back any longer. He sank deeply into her until he couldn't go any deeper, then his hips began to hammer as he invaded her time and again, and the pain in her voice disappeared and he heard only pleasure.

There was a certain madness to be found in her silky body, a certain ecstasy. Once again, he pushed into her as hard and as deep as he could, and she took him, adjusting, accepting, until her climax began, rippling around him. It was too much for him. He came apart, exploding inside her, emptying himself, and filling his heart and soul up with her.

———————————————

"You were a virgin," Jonah said, some minutes later. He was raised up on one elbow.

"Yes."

"How? Why?"

She couldn't resist reaching up to his face to touch him. The ceiling fan above them sent air dancing over their naked bodies, but his skin was hot. "I told you. I spend a lot of time alone."

"But—"

Her fingers slipped over his lips, quieting him. "Does it matter?"

He took her hand in his. "No. Yes."

"Good answer," she whispered. "It covers all the bases."

He groaned at himself. "I can't tell you how happy I am to be the first, Jolie, but I'm surprised."

She moved impatiently. "Do we have to talk about this?"

He was silent for a moment. "Are you all right?"

"Absolutely."

Concern etched his hard face. "But I hurt you."

"Only at first." She entwined her fingers with his, then she brought their joined hands downward until they rested on her waist, the back of his hand touching her skin.

"There are volumes I don't know about you," he said gruffly, "but I just learned something about you that I'm willing to bet no one else knows. And," he murmured as he bent to kiss her, "it's a start."

Be satisfied for now, she wanted to say to him. Don't probe or pry. Let me do what I have to do. And maybe, just maybe, we can have some more time together. Returning his kiss, she caressed his cheek, understanding that she wasn't thinking about forever. Forever was a concept she couldn't let herself think about.

EIGHT

As darkness faded from the sky and the gray of dawn's first light appeared, Jolie reluctantly eased away from the warmth of Jonah's big body and slid from the bed, leaving behind the smell of sex and of him.

It didn't take her too long to find her clothes and dress. Then she crept from the house, gathered the paintings and her backpack from behind the hedges, and made her way to her car.

Jonah would probably never know the price she had to pay for leaving without waking him. Her body had become so accustomed to his in the night, her skin so sensitized to him, that the separation caused her physical pain. There was nothing she'd like more than to initiate further lovemaking. But she had no choice. If she allowed much more time to pass before she left, she ran the risk that the paintings could be discovered. A sizable estate like Jonah's would most assuredly have one or more gardeners who no doubt began their work early.

As she drove home, Jonah and what had happened between them filled her thoughts. She regretted nothing, absolutely nothing. Almost from their first kiss, they had been on the verge of making love. In the end it had been inevitable.

All through the night he had taught her about passion. He had shown her its power, its strength, and incredibly, its gentleness. And while he was doing it he had imprinted himself on her so thoroughly, no amount of time would ever cause his memory to fade from her mind, no amount of soap and water would ever eradicate his scent from her skin. Jonah was her destiny, but whether or not they would be together much longer remained to be seen.

It was a new day, and she still had her father to protect. He was her first priority, by choice, by necessity. And because that was so, she had to continue to deceive Jonah.

In the night she had trusted her body to him and been vastly rewarded. He hadn't asked her to trust him with her heart and she was sure he wouldn't. But she knew with absolute certainty that the one thing she couldn't trust him with was the knowledge of what her father had done. She simply couldn't risk it. Because if he chose, he could destroy her father.

"Papa?" After arriving home, she had showered and changed and then gone in search of her father. She found him in his studio, staring hard at a practice canvas. It stood on an easel next to one that held a vivid, almost animated painting by Cézanne of a vase of flowers. Jolie's heart sank. "What are you doing? I didn't know that you had received a new commission."

"Yes, yes, I did."

She walked closer and peered at the practice canvas. He was working on only a small section of the painting, a grouping of petals. "Papa?"

"You were right," he said dully. "I can't do it anymore. I can't."

The statement was so unlike her father, she wasn't certain what he meant. "Does this mean you're stopping?"

"I have to."

She didn't bother to hide her sigh of relief. She gave him a quick hug. "Thank God you've realized and admitted that you can't do it anymore. You don't know how happy you've made me." Maybe now the two of them could lead a more normal life. Maybe now she could actually have a chance for a real relationship with Jonah.

"I can't do it anymore," he repeated. "But now the world will know."

Jolie's feeling of relief disappeared, replaced by a cold dread. "Know what?"

"I'm going to tell the world what I've been doing for the past six years. Finally everyone will recognize my genius for what it is."

Her knees went weak, but sitting was out of the question. She took him by the shoulders and turned him to her. "What are you talking about? If you tell *anyone*, you will be recognized for a *thief*, not a genius."

"No, no, you don't understand. You've never understood. When they realize the masterpieces they've been in awe of, whether it be a Monet or a Renoir or whatever, are actually *my* work, they are going to be in raptures over me."

"Raptures." She felt as if she'd been hit in the stomach. "And the real Renoirs and Monets that you have in your basement vault? What about them?"

He gave an airy wave of his hand. "They will be given back, of course. I never meant to keep them, you know that. But they won't matter, don't you see? *My* work will be what matters."

She stared at him in horror. She had been so busy covering his tracks that it had never once occurred to her that he would think of actually revealing, in fact *boasting* of, what he had done.

Was this all her fault? she wondered. Because of her efforts, he had been able to stay out of jail. And since he had no idea that she'd been following along behind him, cleaning up after him, he believed that his forgeries had gone undetected all these years. Consequently, his belief in his artistry had grown until it was out of all proportion.

He didn't know that it was his forgeries that were in the basement vault and that the real works of art were hanging exactly where they should be hanging. He didn't know that if he told what he'd done, the authorities would rush to authenticate the paintings, and when they found they were the originals, he would look a fool. It would be worse than prison for him.

She had no choice. She was going to have to tell him what she'd done. It would be a severe blow to his pride, but at least it would keep him from humiliating himself.

"Dad . . ." She heard the distant whir of a helicopter, and as she listened, the noise of the blades beating through the air grew louder and louder. *Jonah.*

A glance at her father told her he wasn't hearing the sound. His gaze had returned to the canvas on which he had been attempting to duplicate Cézanne's flower petals. "Dad, what do you have planned for today?"

"Planned?" His brow wrinkled, but he didn't answer her.

"You're not going anywhere, are you?"

"I don't think so."

"Good. I have someone coming to see me, but after the person leaves, I'm going to make a doctor's appointment for you." She pressed a kiss to his cheek. "Why don't you try to get some rest before lunch, and I'll talk to you after my friend leaves. Okay?"

He gave an absent nod. "Sure."

From the sound of it, Jonah had landed his helicopter. With one last look at her father, she went to greet Jonah, anticipation shimmering through her.

Jonah secured the helicopter, then climbed from the craft. It was then he saw her, walking toward him across the field. She was wearing a long loose flowered dress, and her honey-brown hair was soft around her face. With the warm sunlight on her bare arms and legs, she looked luminous. He drank in the sight.

He met her in the middle of the field, and without saying a word drew her into his arms for a long kiss. Mild shock coursed through him. Until he had felt her in his arms, until his mouth had met hers, he hadn't realized how badly he'd needed to see her again.

He tightened his hold on her, lifted her off the ground against him, and slowly turned. At this moment there was no one else who mattered. They could have been in the middle of a busy intersection and his reaction to her would have been the same. His need for her thrummed through him, strong and vital. Everything in him was centered on her.

He ended the kiss only because he wanted to talk to her. Reluctantly he put her down.

The breeze ruffled through her hair and played with the hem of her skirt. She laughed, a light, silvery, delighted sound. "Well, hello. What are you doing here?"

He tilted his head to one side, listening. "I don't think I've ever heard you laugh before, at least not like that."

"Like what?" Despite her problems with her father, she was absurdly happy to see Jonah again. Excitement wound like a bright ribbon through her, bringing her to glittering life. It was impossible to be casual about anything when he was around.

"Um, joyous, I think." Unable to resist the lure of the softness of her lips, he bent his head and kissed her once again, this time briefer, but with no less feeling. When he raised his head, his eyes were very dark, and when he spoke, his voice was a growl. "I can't seem to get enough of you, which brings me to one of the reasons why I'm here. I really *hated* waking up to find you gone."

She took a step away from him in an attempt to break away from his magnetism. "I had things to do and the drive back here was long."

"There were ways around that. I could have flown you here and made arrangements for your car to be delivered. All you had to do was tell me."

"There was no point in waking you."

Slivers of dark emotion entered his eyes as he gripped her arms. "There was *every* point, Jolie. I went to sleep with you in my arms, and that's damn well the way I wanted to wake up."

Surprisingly she didn't feel the need to tread carefully in the face of his intimidating intensity, perhaps because she had experienced the zenith of that intensity in the night and had thrived on it. She smiled. "Let me get this straight. You're angry with me and you flew here to tell me so. Right?"

His grip on her arms eased. "Yes, I'm angry with you, and yes, I wanted to tell you, and no, that's not the only reason I flew here."

Her smile broadened. Truthfully he was just annoyed that things hadn't gone entirely his way. In light of what they had shared in the night, she supposed she could see his point, but with everything that was on her mind, it didn't seem significant. "Then why don't we skip ahead to the other reasons?"

He frowned. "You're not taking me seriously, are you?"

"I take you very seriously, Jonah," she said, and meant every word.

No, she didn't, he thought, not on the particular issue of her leaving without waking him, because she didn't understand the extent of *his* seriousness. Hell, he didn't entirely understand. He simply knew he had felt a tremendous disappointment when he'd awakened and found her gone. And he hadn't questioned his instincts to climb into the helicopter and direct it toward her house.

Even now he felt the white-hot heat of desire rise in him. He wanted her in every way, but he didn't even have her whole attention. His goal was to get her to want him as much as he wanted her, and he wouldn't stop until he had succeeded. "Okay, then, since we're obviously not going to agree on that point, let's get to my other reasons for coming. One of them was to see you and kiss you good morning."

She smiled. "Which you've done."

"Which I've done," he said with a nod. "And another reason was to see your paintings."

Her smile faded. "You want to see my paintings?"

"Why is that such a surprise? I made a verbal offer to buy three of them a few days ago."

"A very foolish offer. You made it without
knowing what you're buying."

"Then show me."

Various thoughts flew through her mind as
she considered his request. In truth, the reason
for her initial objection no longer mattered.
She'd been trying to guard herself against him,
but he hadn't allowed that and she hadn't been
able to hold out against him. They had been
intimate. There were many things he didn't
know about her, might never know, but, she
concluded, it was absurd and pointless of her
to try to keep him from seeing her work. "All
right." She turned and began walking back
toward the house and he fell into step beside
her.

"Is your father here?" he asked. "I'd like to
say hello."

"That's very nice of you, but he's not feeling well. He's resting." She would have liked
to think that he was resting, but she knew he
wasn't. He was probably still sitting in front of
the damn canvas, staring at what he viewed as
his inadequacies.

"I'm sorry to hear he's not feeling well."

"So am I. I'm taking him to the doctor this
afternoon."

"Then it's serious?"

"No, I don't think so. I hope not. It's just time he had a checkup."

He reached for her hand, enfolding her smaller one in his. "Well, I'm doubly sorry you have to take him to the doctor, because I had plans to lure you out of your house today to come spend some time with me."

"Lure?" She turned her head toward him and the breeze blew her hair across her eyes.

He reached out and brushed her hair away. "Wouldn't you like to be lured?"

Her mouth twisted wryly. "As I recall, I have been lured. Last night, as a matter of fact."

He threw back his head and laughed. "I recall that too. Vividly." He tugged on her hand, stopping her. "I enjoyed the hell out of it," he said, his voice low now, all laughter gone. "And I want to be with you tonight. I'll fly over and pick you up whenever you say."

"You're going to be home tonight?" She asked the question, though the answer didn't matter. The job had to be done. She was simply going to have to switch the paintings while he was asleep in the house. It would be tricky, but her real challenge was going to be the security system.

"Yes, and I want you there with me."

"I'm not sure. . . ." She should say no, then make the drive to his place after midnight and wait for her opportunity. The time was growing shorter and shorter.

And she *couldn't* spend the night, make love with him, *and* switch the paintings, not on the same night. To ease her conscience even a little, she'd had to divide the two things in her mind. Making love to Jonah could have nothing to do with the job she had to do because of her father. "Let me wait and see what the doctor says about Papa."

He lifted her hand to his lips. "May he have a very clean bill of health, because I don't know how long I can go without having you again."

A thrill shivered through her, but without saying anything more, she led the way into the house. Her studio was in a different portion of the house from her father's, reached by climbing two sets of staircases to the top floor.

She opened the door into a room filled with windows and sunlight. It smelled of turpentine and paint and held what seemed to Jonah hundreds of canvases, stacked in an orderly fashion against the walls, face out. She closed the door behind them, then leaned back against it, issuing him an unspoken invitation to explore.

Even though Winston had told him she had talent, he was unprepared for the extent of it. He'd never seen anything like her technique. Basically, she wove fresh, innovative pictures with painted lines as if she were creating a tapestry, actually painting in the warp and woof of thread. It appeared as if she layered wet colors on wet, mixing the colors on the canvas and not on a palette, so that the colors changed from one to another right before the viewer's eyes. She took straight lines and made them something more.

"You are amazing," he said almost to himself.

"Thank you," she said, still leaning against the door.

He studied several more paintings then turned to her, his eyes blazing with anger. "Why in the hell aren't you putting these paintings out so that people can see them?"

"I do."

"I'm not talking about the few Winston can get out of you. I'm talking about doing what artists do. Mount exhibitions. Get publicity. Sell."

"I don't need the acclaim or the money."

"There are ways to avoid becoming a public person—hire a publicist to keep your name *out* of the public's eyes. And if money is so abhorrent to you, give it to charity. But for goodness' sake, put your paintings out there. They deserve to be seen and appreciated."

She smiled faintly. "You make one pass

around my studio and decide my whole life needs changing."

"Dammit, Jolie, I'm not talking about your whole life. I'm simply talking about—"

"My whole life."

He exhaled slowly. She was right, but he wasn't ready to admit it yet. "I suppose it might mean a certain amount of adjustment on your part."

"Yes, it would."

"But there are ways of doing it. I don't understand—"

She held up a hand. "Look, Jonah. I may not feel the same way in five years. Or ten years. And if I don't, I can change things then. But for now I like my life just fine the way it is."

He walked back to her. "And you won't even talk about it?"

"Talk about it, Jonah? You mean, talk about it until you change my mind? It's not going to happen."

"So you're telling me I'm defeated in this matter?"

She smiled. "I wouldn't have used the word *defeated*, but, yes, you are."

He placed his hands beside her head against the door and leaned his body to hers. "You will make room in your life for me, though."

She smiled again, the humor more unchecked this time. "Let's see—was that a question, a request, or an order?"

"It was a plea," he said, pressing his body down on hers so he could feel the swell of her breasts pushing into his chest. "And a demand."

He threaded his hand through her silky hair and crushed his mouth down on hers. As her mouth softened beneath his, yielded, he felt himself come alive in the same way he did every time he kissed her. She made him aware as he'd never been before, aware of the blood heating and thickening in his veins. Of the tightening of his groin and the swelling of his arousal. Of the air he breathed, which was filled with her. She made him aware of each beat of his heart and of the emptiness there when he wasn't with her. As if the feeling were a drug, he wasn't certain he could ever again do without it.

Abruptly he broke off the kiss, because he knew if he didn't, he would take her right there on the floor of her studio. Even though he'd relish making love to her anywhere, no matter the discomfort or awkwardness, she deserved more consideration.

He framed her face with his hands and gazed down into her eyes. "If your father is very ill, I'll hire a nurse to stay with him tonight, but I want you with me."

She needed to tell him no. The sooner she

switched the paintings, the sooner she'd be able to get on with the rest of her life. But with the heat from his kiss still running rampant through her system, she was weak. "Maybe."

He rubbed his pelvis against hers. "Feel that? I need you, Jolie. You have no idea how much."

And to her surprise, she needed him, and not just to make love to. She felt an over-whelming need to have him hold her all through the night. She'd spent the last six years of her life since her mother died trying *not* to need anyone, but surely one night of being needy wouldn't hurt anything. And surely it would be all right if she waited one more night to switch the paintings. She was unaccustomed to putting herself before her father and the need to protect him. But just this once . . .

"I'll call you after I've talked with the doctor," she said.

It took a lot of talking and cajoling to get her father to the doctor. It made her realize that the only reason he had taken her previous mentions of the doctor so well was because he hadn't heard her. By the time they returned home, she was exhausted. All she wanted to do was climb into her bed and fall asleep. But when she called Jonah to tell him that she wasn't going to see him, she never got the words out. She heard his deep growl of a voice and knew she needed him more than rest.

"Come get me," she said.

And within thirty minutes his helicopter was landing in the meadow.

NINE

Jonah brushed his fingers over her hair. She felt the gesture all the way through her body. He had arranged for a light supper of wine, cheese, bread, and fruit to be served in a room smaller than the salon, cozier. But it, too, was on the first floor, with doors that opened onto a side terrace, and a fireplace where he had started a fire, even though it was a mild spring night.

As she had eaten, Jonah had talked, about nothing really. He mentioned a family of rabbits he'd come upon in the garden that afternoon, and his cousin's daughter Lily, and how adorable she was. The subjects seemed to be chosen without intent or underlying purpose, but were meant, she knew, to put her at ease. And to a certain extent it was working.

"Jolie?" Beside her on the couch, he once

again lifted his hand to stroke her hair. "You seem distracted tonight. What's wrong? You did say your father was okay, didn't you?"

"He's fine, all things considered." The whole way home from the doctor's he'd grumbled to himself about wasted time, and when they arrived, he'd gone straight to his studio.

"And it was nothing serious, right?"

"Fortunately no. He has high blood pressure, which we didn't know, but it can be controlled with medication." She made a face. "All I have to do is get him to remember to take it. The rest is simply the vagaries of getting older. The body changes."

"And that's it?"

"Just about." The doctor said they would keep an eye on the problem of his shaking hands.

"Okay," he said, regarding her thoughtfully, "but is there some reason you're still worried about him? Your mind seems a million miles away."

Lies and deceptions. She could simply tell Jonah she wasn't worried about her father, but it would be a lie. And she found herself wanting to tell him the truth, at least as much as she could. "I have been worried about him. He's all I have now, and I'm all he has. I try to look out for him."

"You said your mother died six years ago?" he asked quietly.

"When I was twenty." She paused. "They were madly in love with each other." She smiled, remembering. "*Madly*. When I was a little girl, I used to watch them together. As young as I was, I could see the love between them. What I didn't see until later was that she was his strength. As long as he had her, he could tolerate the world."

"Tolerate the world?" His brow lifted. "Granted I've met him only once, but your father seemed as if he were tolerating the world pretty well."

Because his work was being praised, she thought ruefully. "Under certain circumstances, he does pretty well, most particularly when it involves his work. It's the other times I try to look out for. From the day of my mother's funeral, the light seemed to go out of him."

"But what about you? He still had you."

Her lips curved faintly. "Yes, and he loves me very much. I honestly think that if it were necessary, he wouldn't hesitate to lay down his life for me. But as long as I'm healthy and functioning, he retreats into his own world and doesn't come out for days at a time."

Jonah frowned. There was something bothering her that she wasn't telling him. He had been aware from the first that she kept things from him, but it was something he hadn't been able to accept. "But now that you know he's healthy, you can quit worrying, right?"

If she only could. But when he had informed her that he was going to go public with his forgeries, he had presented her with a problem she hadn't foreseen, and she hadn't figured out yet how she was going to deal with it. "Some habits are hard to break."

"Well, for tonight, try not to worry. I want your full attention."

She looked at him in surprise. "You've got it."

"No, I don't think so. But I'm willing to work on it."

Warmth stirred in her and a deep sweetness. Because there was a great deal weighing on her, she sometimes forgot how very much she had grown to care about Jonah. She brushed her fingertips across his cheekbones. "I think your shadows are fading. You must be getting more rest."

"I didn't last night."

Faint color climbed beneath her skin, but she smiled. "I remember. But if it's not the rest, then something is making the shadows fade."

"Maybe it's you."

She shook her head. "I'm sure I haven't had a thing in the world to do with it."

With a hand along her jaw, he turned her face to his. "Since the moment I met you I haven't drawn a breath that hasn't involved you. I think I'm falling in love with you."

"*No.*"

His mouth curved slightly. "Really interesting response, Jolie, but it doesn't change what I'm feeling."

"I—I'm sorry. It's just that you took me by surprise."

"It's taken me by surprise too." He saw the wariness in her eyes, the guardedness, and almost cursed aloud. He didn't regret telling her what he was feeling, but he wished he knew why she felt the need to keep a part of herself separate from him.

"You said you *think* you are falling in love with me."

"Yes, I think I am, I believe I am. I've never fallen in love before, but I seem to have all the symptoms—like I can't stand it when I'm away from you, and when I'm with you I don't want to let you out of my sight."

She recognized the symptoms because she had them, too, but even though she'd admitted to herself that she cared deeply about him, she'd never once considered that she might love him. Love, it seemed to her, was totally different. It would involve a whole other set of rules, rules that would mean complete commitment, complete truth. She didn't know how, and she didn't think she could afford to let herself learn right now. "You know, we really haven't known each other that long at all."

"Ah, Jolie." He sifted her hair through his fingers. "You do fascinate me, you really do. I tell you I think I'm falling in love with you and you try to talk me out of it."

"The thing is, there are so many other women who would love to hear you say that."

"And you're telling me this because . . . why? You'd like me to tell one of them that I love her?"

"No." Even the thought made her heart ache.

He sighed. "I'm sorry. I've frightened you."

Yes, he had. "We do seem to be going awfully fast."

"It's all right," he said softly, leaning forward to brush a kiss across her mouth. "Take your time. I'm going to be here. But I *am* falling in love with you. Every instinct I have is telling me that it's true, and my instincts never fail me."

She had instincts, too, along with a lot of common sense, and they were all telling her she had to proceed with extreme caution.

"More wine?" he asked.

"No thank you," she said, gazing into the flickering fire.

"Then," he said in the low growl that

never failed to heat her nerves, "let's go to bed."

The curtains blew into the bedroom with the breeze. Moonlight spilled across the floor and onto the bed. His skin was hot and sweaty beneath her touch, his muscles tight and bunched. He was deep inside her, hard and throbbing. And each time he withdrew and sank into her again, a sharp pleasure pierced through her.

She'd never understood that such feelings existed. Never known that a man was capable of using strength and power as well as tenderness and gentleness. Never known that the mere act of lovemaking would require so much from her. There were times she felt as if she were dissolving, times she felt as if she were exploding.

This was the second time he had taken her tonight. The first time had been fast and hard and incredibly satisfying. This time was slow and languorous, with him leaving no part of her untouched, inside or out. He was using his hands, his fingers, his mouth, his sex. He knew her well now, knew exactly how to make her moan or whimper or cry out with ecstasy.

His big hands gripped her hips as he drove into her again, shaking her body with the force and power of his thrust. White-hot pleasure scored through her, and she pressed her mouth against his shoulder and hung on to him with all her strength.

As he thrust into her again he threaded his fingers through her hair and tugged, pulling her head back so that he could look down into her eyes. "Talk to me," he muttered as he pushed in and out of her. "Tell me again how you don't love me. Tell me again how we're going too fast. And then tell me to stop."

She gave a little cry and grabbed for his hips, feeling the strength of his muscles as they flexed. "No, don't stop."

A deep laugh rumbled up from his chest, then he pressed his mouth to her ear. "You're going to love me, Jolie. You're going to love me."

Tears filled her eyes. He had taken over her body, filling her with sensations so pure, so volatile, she wasn't certain she'd be able to endure them. With every stroke, the need coiled tighter and tighter until it was almost pain. She lifted her hips up to him and gasped when he thrust deeper into her.

He smoothed her damp hair off her face as once more he slid into her, but this time slower and with less force. As her body eased back from the peak she gave a sob of disappointment. "Jonah."

She could feel his muscles quivering, his heart pounding. The fact that he wanted her as badly as she wanted him didn't assuage the aching and need that went clear through her bones. "Do you want me to beg?" she asked in a pain-laced whisper.

"I thought I did," he whispered back, shuddering compulsively. "But you defeat me." With a swift movement he buried himself inside her as deeply as he could. He wanted her too much to deny himself for long. Holding back was no longer an alternative. There was a fire deep in his belly that wouldn't be put out. He slammed into her again and again, shaking the bed, shaking her, shaking him. And when she stiffened and cried out, he couldn't even pause. She was tight and hot and everything he'd ever wanted. And he couldn't get his fill. He loved her and he would want her forever.

Sometime in the night he awoke to find her lying over him, her mouth filled with him, her tongue working magic. Her perfume mingled with the scent of sex and desire in his nostrils. The breeze was cool, but her skin was hot and so was he, with the eternal fire in his belly burning for her. With a groan, he held her head as she lavished great attention on him, and he found he could do nothing except surrender himself and drown in the endless waves of pleasure that kept coming at him.

———◆——————◆———

"You're never going to get away from me," he murmured as the dawn broke outside the windows. She was lying with her face on his broad chest, and his fingers were threaded through her tangled hair.

She listened to his voice rumble in his chest as he spoke. She heard his heart beat, strong and steady beneath her ear. Their night together had been exhilarating, erotic, amazing. She'd give anything for it not to end. She'd give anything not to have to say what she was about to. "Jonah?"

"Mmm?"

"Remember when I told you that I was going to be busy for two weeks?"

"Mmm." His fingers idly played in her hair.

"Well, I'm not going to be able to see you for a few days."

She could almost feel each of his muscles as they tensed, and she wanted to cry.

"Why?"

"I still have some things I have to take care of."

"So many things that you can't see me, even in the evening?"

"That's right."

He jackknifed upright, the movement forcing her to get out of his way and sit up. They were both naked, but she didn't even think about reaching for a sheet. She was too concerned with his reaction.

His eyes had turned to stone. "Where are you going to sleep? Or should I ask, with whom?"

"Don't say that, Jonah. There is no one else. You should know that. You were the first man who ever made love to me. You're the only."

He didn't relax, not a bit. "Then *why*?"

"I can't explain everything. Not now. But I have to do something for my father."

"Then let me help."

"You can't." Her tongue flicked out and made a nervous sweep of her bottom lip. "Look, it may not even take several days. I may be able to accomplish what I have to do quicker. But it won't be long, I promise."

"But where will you be? Will we be able to talk by phone?"

"No. I'm going to be too busy."

He stared at her, wondering how he was going to survive without her, even for a few days. Her hair was a tangled cloud around her head, the hair he had gripped and tugged on during the height of passion. And her lips were swollen from the countless times he'd kissed her and she'd kissed him. And her tongue . . . During the night they had made love every way there was and still it hadn't been enough.

The thought of not seeing her made him want to scream.

With a movement too quick for her to anticipate, he pushed her down onto the bed until she lay flat on her back, and covered her smaller body with his big one. "I don't understand what you're saying, and I don't like it. But you're here with me now and I don't want to waste one minute arguing with you."

He parted her thighs and entered her, claiming her in the only way he could for now. And she accepted him with a deep moan of pleasure.

"Papa, I want you to listen to me carefully." She had found him in his studio, working on the cleaning of the Cézanne. And she was relieved to see that the practice canvas had been set aside on the floor.

He shot her an irritated look. "I can hear you fine, Jolie Christiane. What is it you want me to hear?"

"Would you please come sit down?" She patted the paint-splattered cushion next to the one she sat on. The last time the couch had been reupholstered, her mother had done it, and even though the material was faded and torn, she knew her father would never consent to having it replaced. "I really need your full attention."

With obvious reluctance and ill temper, he laid down his brush, perched himself on a tall stool he rarely sat on, and folded his arms across his chest. She was immediately reminded of a recalcitrant child.

With a sigh she rubbed her forehead. "All right, Papa, here it is. You cannot go public with the knowledge that you've been switching the original paintings with your own, because I've been putting the originals back."

He stared at her as if she'd just uttered Greek.

"It's true," she said.

Slowly his expression turned stricken. He opened his mouth, but no words came out.

Concerned, she jumped up and handed him the bottle of water he always kept by his side when he worked. "Take a drink," she said, and waited while he complied. "I had to do it, Papa. Otherwise you would have been caught and sent to prison. I couldn't have that and you wouldn't stop. I had to do something."

"But—but the basement vault. There are paintings down there."

"They're yours."

"All of them?"

She nodded.

"You went behind my back and replaced *all of them*?" His tone was incredulous, filled with hurt and betrayal.

"Yes, Papa, I did."

"But that can't be. I mean, how could you?"

He didn't want to believe it, she thought. "I broke into the homes of the people who owned the paintings. Thank God you took commissions only from the private sector. I'm not sure I could have managed museums. And thank God you made only one or two forgeries a year."

"You broke into their homes? No." He shook his head. "Those people have top-notch security, dogs."

"I became an expert in just about every kind of security system there is. And I learned how to handle dogs."

He shifted on the stool. "You shouldn't have done it. It was a lot of trouble and fuss for no reason. If I'd known, I would have stopped you."

"But would you have stopped making the forgeries? Because that's all you would have had to do to stop me."

He thought for a minute. "When did you start replacing the paintings?"

She silently sighed. Getting him to accept what she had done was harder than she had thought. And now his mind had taken another tack. For years she'd handled him with kid gloves, unable to get through to him. He left her with no choice. As much as she hated to do it, as fearful as she was of the consequences to her father, she had to shock him out of the fog he lived in.

"I started replacing the paintings as soon as you began to do it, with your first commission after Mother died."

"The Cummings?"

She nodded. "And since then I've been *committing crimes to protect you.*"

"Don't be silly." He waved a hand dismissively. "You haven't committed any crimes. All you've done is give people back what was theirs in the first place."

"If I had been discovered, charges could have been pressed against me for breaking and entering and possession of stolen goods. I could have been sent to prison."

Alarm entered her father's eyes. "Prison? But—"

"What do you think would have happened if one of those people whose home I was breaking into heard me make a noise? If they had a gun, they probably would have come after me and shot me. I could have died, Papa. I could have *died.*"

He paled. "No, no . . ."

Fear lanced through Jolie. Had she pushed her father too far? She was all set to rush to him to comfort him, but to her amazement, his terror faded and comprehension dawned over him. It was something she hadn't witnessed since her mother had died.

His expression now filled with a wealth of sadness and regret. "Jolie Christiane. How could I not have seen what I was doing to you?"

Her relief was instantaneous. This time she did rush to him and embrace him. She'd worked so hard and was now so close to succeeding completely in her effort to keep her father safe. He'd finally seen the light. And she was finally seeing a chance at happiness with Jonah.

Jolie crouched in the darkness about twenty-five yards from the back of Jonah's house. The three paintings were strapped to her back, the backpack with her tools was over her shoulders.

She glanced again at the luminous dial of her watch. Four-thirty in the morning. It had been an hour since she had seen the lights in Jonah's bedroom go off. She couldn't afford to wait any longer.

She started off. There were two separate alarm systems, one for the house and one for the salon, both state-of-the-art. It would take every ounce of ingenuity, expertise, and strength she possessed to disarm them.

It was amazing how tiring it was to be still when it was required, to be precise when it was needed. It was amazing how much energy it took to concentrate fully. And to do it, she had to block everything from her mind, including the fact that this was Jonah's home and that he was probably at this minute upstairs, lying in the bed they had made love in. But nothing could matter except her task.

All her senses were wide-awake, her body completely attuned to what she was doing, her touch super-sensitive to the point she could feel the slightest vibration around her. At times it seemed she was concentrating so hard, she was in a different state of consciousness, an altered state where there were only the alarms and her.

Working in the dark with a flashlight, she made it past the alarm system for the house, and then finally through the system for the salon. A clock ticked somewhere. A tree branch scratched against a window. The first two paintings were replaced in no time.

Sweat beading her forehead, she started to replace the last painting in its frame. Just a little more time . . .

Light flooded the room.

She froze, momentarily blinded. Then slowly her eyes adjusted and she saw Jonah standing in the doorway, wearing only a pair of jeans. In a matter of seconds a myriad of emotions crossed his face.

"Jolie?" His smile of happiness at seeing her was almost instantly replaced by confusion, followed rapidly by the stark horror of realization as his gaze focused on the paintings on the floor by her knees. "What in the . . . ?"

Slowly she came to her feet. "Jonah, I can explain."

His face went expressionless, but dark fury blazed in his eyes. "Explain? Or lie?"

She'd thought him hard before; she'd thought him capable of cruelty and violence. She'd thought him dangerous. But she hadn't begun to guess at the extent of what he would be like when crossed. There was a stillness in his body, a control, that spoke of a killing rage just beneath the surface. And it froze her to her bones.

"Listen to me, Jonah. Let me explain."

His hand sliced upward, the gesture cutting off her words. His gaze raked her, taking in the all-black clothes she was wearing. "Nice outfit, Jolie. I remember thinking it was nice the other night too. The night we made love for the first time." His voice was soft, each word a sliver of ice.

"Jonah—"

He advanced toward her, the muscles in his big lean body tensed as if he were about to attack. "You were trying to break into my house that night, weren't you? If I hadn't heard you, or if I hadn't been home, you would have broken in and stolen the paintings."

"I'm not stealing from you, Jonah."

He stopped in front of her. A vein beat in his forehead, but his voice was hushed. "I've spent the last few years living a life where trust was nonexistent, where if I assumed the worst of a person, I was always right. And then I came home. I felt safe. I met you and never once thought about caution. How incredibly stupid of me. And the irony is that I was so afraid you wouldn't trust me, while all along I shouldn't have been trusting you. I fell in love with you and you betrayed me."

"*No.* I didn't betray you. Not really." He ever so lightly brushed his fingers down the side of her cheek and she felt as if he'd hit her.

"Then what would you call breaking into my house and trying to steal my paintings? A gesture of respect and love?"

"I was trying to put your paintings *back*. Just listen to me for a minute." Tears filled her eyes. "I would never hurt you, Jonah."

Something was tearing apart inside him. He felt sick to his stomach. "You *used* me, damn you."

He wasn't listening. "No, no, I didn't. I—"

"You used me to get into my house."

His words sliced at her, sharp enough to cut. Enough of them, she thought, and she might bleed to death. "*Think*, Jonah. I broke in tonight after I thought you were asleep. If I—"

His harsh laugh splintered apart until there was nothing left but the sound of pain. "I couldn't sleep because I was thinking of you. Another irony, huh? And then I came down and here you were. A hell of a wish fulfillment, right? I'd say something definitely got twisted along the way."

His anger and hurt were coming at her in waves, suffocating her. She couldn't take any more. She gripped his arms and tried to shake him, but his big body didn't move. "Jonah, I didn't use you. If I'd wanted to use you, I would have stayed with you tonight, and then when you were asleep I would have slipped down here and switched the paintings. Or I would have done it that first night. But I didn't."

"Switched them?" He barely glanced at the art on the floor. "So if I hadn't found you here tonight, I would never have known that I had been robbed because you were replacing them with fakes. I wouldn't have known, that is, under normal circumstances." Abruptly he shrugged her hands off him. "But I was about to ship them out on tour, and as a matter of routine they're scheduled to be authenticated. I would have known I'd been robbed then, but I wouldn't have known who or how or even when." His mouth twisted into a cruel slant. "Would you have been at my side then, Jolie? Offering me sympathy and consolation with sugar-filled words and kisses? Or would you have been long gone by then, concentrating on your next victim?"

She fought hard to keep her voice steady. "If you hadn't found me tonight and stopped me, you still would have been told that your paintings are the original masterpieces."

"Are your forgeries that good?"

"I don't make forgeries." She stopped herself before she could go any further. She'd spent years protecting her father and it was an ingrained habit she couldn't break.

"No? You have an accomplice? I should have known." He spat the words out. "He's a man, right? Of course. And with his work and your hot body, you've got it made."

"There is no accomplice, Jonah. I was a virgin the first time you and I made love—you know that."

He reached out and rubbed his thumb across her lower lip, using a hard pressure. "So, with me you went one step further than usual. I don't suppose you have to do too much to get a man to fall under your spell. Just smile, get a guy to fall in love with you, and then use him. If he doesn't discover you in the act, he'll never know what hit him. Trust me."

She jerked her head back. "How did I use you, Jonah?" she asked heatedly. "You didn't give me your security code. You didn't give me a key to the front door."

"No," he said, his voice barely above a

whisper. "I simply fell in love with you." Turning, he walked away from her.

She looked after him, her heart breaking. God knew she never meant to hurt him, but she had. If only there was a way to go back and do things differently. But what? How? She'd tried to stay away from him, but she hadn't been able to resist him. She loved him.

She paused in her thoughts. *She loved him.* And she wasn't surprised. Somewhere inside her she'd known all along. But he would never believe her if she told him now.

If Jonah had come into the salon just a couple of minutes later, she would have been home free, without the worry and constant fear that her father would be discovered and put in jail. But she'd been caught.

She remembered thinking that she trusted Jonah with herself, but not with her father's secret. She could keep that secret still. It was an option. But no. Quite simply it was beyond her to lie to him one more time, even by omission. And if she told him the truth, it might in some way lessen his hurt.

Jonah had opened one set of French doors and was standing in the opening with his legs spread, his hands on his hips, the muscles in his back bunched with tension.

"My father made these forgeries. And others." She saw a shudder shake him, then he turned around. "I told you, after my mother died, he became obsessed with his art. Hearing the raves over his forgeries of masterpieces became his one source of pleasure."

"What lie are you telling me now, Jolie?"

"I wish it were a lie. You don't know how much."

She pointed to the two Matisse paintings on the floor. "Those are my father's work. I have already replaced the originals." She gestured to the wall where they hung. "And the Renoir that you caught me working on is the original." She pointed to it. "My father won't be making any more forgeries—he understands that now. Your paintings are the last of them. After tonight it all stops."

"It's a damn good story, Jolie. Very inventive. But how do you expect me to believe you?"

"I don't know," she said, sadness filling her voice. "But for your own peace of mind, get the paintings authenticated."

"Peace of mind, Jolie? Forget it. But don't worry about the authentication. No matter what, I will have that done." He glanced at his wristwatch. "In another hour I'll call someone I know who'll be able to give me at least an initial indication. But it still won't tell me exactly what you were doing."

"Then you're going to have to decide whether or not you can believe me."

"You've got to be kidding." His expression

turned bleak as he gazed at her. "How could I have been so wrong about you?"

"I never lied to you, Jonah."

"But you didn't tell me the whole truth either, did you?"

"No, I didn't."

"And you spent time with me, slept with me, crept beneath my guard, my skin, *used* me."

He kept coming back to that and she didn't know how to change his mind. "I didn't use you. I didn't *need* to use you. I got in here on my own."

He walked back to her, and when he reached her, he stroked his fingers across her hair, as he had so many times before, but this time his hand shook badly. "I remember seeing you for the first time. I remember thinking there was something mysterious about you. I remember thinking I wanted you."

She swallowed against a lump. There was nothing more that she could say to him, she realized. She had told him the truth; she had apologized.

A pulse throbbed at his temple. "You do understand, don't you, that I can call the police and have you put in jail."

"I understand perfectly."

His brows lifted. "Aren't you going to try to talk me out of it?"

"No."

"Oh, come on, Jolie," he said, his tone turning sarcastic. "Rub that luscious body against mine and see what happens. You did it before, and you were so damn good at it too. You never know—I might forget what you've done. For a little while. And if you're very good, maybe I'll forget for longer than that."

She crossed her arms beneath her breasts. "Be angry with me if you need to be, Jonah, but don't be crude."

"Crude?" he drawled. "The idea sounds *inspired* to me."

"I did what I had to do."

"And what's that? Steal? Lie? Deceive? Have sex with me?"

"I did what I had to do to protect my father, and making love to you had nothing to do with that. You of all people should understand about protecting family. Well, that's what I've been trying to do. I haven't hurt you materially. I haven't hurt *anyone* materially. All I was doing was trying to see that you got back what was rightfully yours."

"Oh, is that all? Funny, I thought you were also knifing me in the back."

She let out a long breath. She'd tried to reason with him, but he was in too much pain right now to listen. He couldn't separate what he was feeling personally from what she was telling him. She accepted full blame, but she couldn't think of what else she could do. She was tired and she was dealing with her own pain. And Jonah was a man who saw an enemy and set out to defeat him. When he looked at her, he now saw an enemy.

Wearily she pushed her hair back from her face. "I'm going home."

His head came up. "You're not going anywhere."

"You know where I live. You can find me there."

Cold calculation entered his eyes. "What if I tell you that the only way I'll let you leave is if you make love to me again? Would you?"

"Jonah, I—"

"Oh, come on, Jolie," he said, reaching for her again and bringing her against him. "You could fake it and I might not even notice. You're so damn good at it."

Before she could say anything, he crushed his mouth down on hers with an anger and dark passion that sent her senses reeling. She couldn't struggle. She didn't want to. Quite simply it was heaven to be back in his arms, being kissed by him. And no matter how angry he was, he still wanted her. And she wanted him.

He'd grabbed her to him and kissed her before he'd had a chance to think about it. And Lord help him, he reflected grimly, now that he'd started, he couldn't stop. He wanted to drop with her to the floor and take her right then and there. He wanted to make love to her until she was helpless and clinging to him, until she had no defenses left, no pretenses. He wanted to make love to her until she was begging him for more, until she was stripped naked emotionally. And then he wanted to look into her eyes and see if the lies and betrayal would still be there.

He wanted to do it so much, his gut ached with the need.

Blindly he shoved her away from him and stalked over to the open door. Inhaling deeply, he prayed for control.

Behind him, Jolie retreated to a nearby couch. She knew better than to say anything. He was a man who had reached a breaking point. And it was all because of her.

Suddenly he wheeled away from the door and headed down the length of the salon to the bar. He splashed a healthy portion of whiskey into a glass, then tossed it down his throat. He waited while it burned its way to his stomach, willing it to burn away the pain and disappointment. But it didn't, of course. And the worst part was that he still wanted her, still loved her.

Jolie had never doubted Jonah's power. No one else would have been able to get an art expert to come to his home at the crack of dawn, but Jonah did. It was as simple for him as a phone call and dispatching his helicopter. The expert arrived and authenticated the paintings.

But if she'd hoped that Jonah would soften toward her once he realized she'd been telling the truth, at least about which were the real paintings, she was disappointed.

He had erected a barrier against her. If she couldn't see the barrier, she could feel it. It was cold and hard and impenetrable.

She was used to protecting someone she loved. If she could have seen how to protect Jonah from herself, she would have, she reflected sadly. But she'd hurt him badly and she couldn't figure out a way to fix his hurt. Or to make him trust her again.

Now what? Jonah asked himself as he rubbed a hand over his face. Lord, but he was tired. He glanced at his watch, surprised to see that it was midmorning. He could go long hours without sleep, but one glance at Jolie told him she couldn't. She looked soft and vulnerable, ready to break. It took all of his control to keep from reaching for her. A tremor shook him at the memory of the satin-smooth skin he had caressed so many times before.

He wanted nothing more than to pull her into his arms and kiss her. But he had to remember that she'd managed to do what no other woman had ever done. She'd made him fall in love with her and then had broken his heart.

He'd thought his security system one of the best, without weaknesses, but he hadn't considered *himself* being a weakness. She'd used him, and by doing so had somehow found a way through the system.

It wouldn't happen again. Within the next twenty-four hours he planned to have a new security system in place, one that *no one* could get through.

But what was he going to do about his heart? a quiet voice in his head asked.

Unable to bear the silence any longer, Jolie finally said, "What happens now?"

"Now?"

Mere yards separated them as she sat on the couch and he stood by the bar, but it might as well have been miles. "What about the police? When are you going to contact them about me?"

"I'm not." There was a pause, and when he spoke again, his voice was lower, with a slightly broken quality to it. "I can't."

She shouldn't allow herself to hope, but she had to ask, "Then . . . what about us?"

"Us? I don't believe there can be an us."

She had thought that she was incapable of feeling any more pain than she already did, but his words proved her wrong. "I didn't fake anything with you, Jonah. Nothing. If you believe nothing else, believe that."

"Good-bye, Jolie," he said softly. With a last look at her, he turned and walked out of the salon.

She was exhausted and her legs felt like lead and she'd run out of words to say to him. Going after him would be pointless. Helplessly she watched him leave, thinking that she couldn't have envisioned this ending for them. Rage and shouting and things breaking apart, yes. But not this, not this deep, quiet pain and sadness that lay between them, with *her* breaking apart.

What was she going to do?

TEN

Jolie crouched in the darkness at the back of Jonah's estate. It was four o'clock in the morning and the lights in his bedroom were off, but she knew he was there. She'd seen him come out on the balcony about two. She'd seen him light a cigar and stand for a long time at the railing while he smoked it. She'd seen him pace back and forth the length of the balcony, then sit. After about an hour he'd returned to his room and the lights had gone out.

She'd been incredibly happy to see him again, even from a distance. As far as she'd been able to tell, he hadn't been home for several nights, and she couldn't help but wonder where he'd been.

He had a new security system. She'd hoped he would get one.

When she'd first encountered it several

nights before, she had been elated and not at all surprised. By breaching his security the first time, she had made him feel vulnerable, exposed. By having the new system installed, he was trying to make sure no one could ever again break into his home without him knowing it.

She'd spent the last few days and nights researching the new system. Whoever had designed it had done an incredible job, taking the best of the best and incorporating them into one. There were features she'd never seen before, never heard of, and there was a chance she wasn't going to be able to get through it. But it was a chance she had to take.

Jonah rolled from his stomach to his back and rubbed his eyes with the heels of his hands. Lack of sleep had left them feeling like sandpaper. And now, even when he was completely exhausted from days crammed with as much activity as he could manage and nights spent without sleep, he still couldn't get comfortable. Nothing was right. The sheets were too wrinkled, the fabric too coarse. Even the ceiling fan was moving too slowly. He was hot and couldn't get cool. He ached all over with a pain that no amount of aspirin could ease.

He stared at the ceiling, remembering that he'd tried to pick a fight with practically every one of his cousins at least once in the last few days. They had wisely ignored him, because they had known, as he slowly figured out, that he was fighting himself.

He'd lost Jolie and he had no one to blame but himself.

Lord, he had been such a fool, walking away from her the way he had. But his pride had been damaged and he'd been hurting so much, he couldn't see or think straight.

That very night he'd flown to Hong Kong to see if he could help Sin, but his main purpose had been to get as far away from Jolie as possible.

Distance hadn't helped. It hadn't been able to quiet the noise in his head or ease the ache in his heart. And it hadn't been able to separate him from Jolie. Every word she'd spoken, every laugh she'd laughed, every small little cry of passion she'd uttered haunted him.

In the end, Sin had told him he had two choices. Either fly home and work things out with Jolie or Sin would put him in a hospital.

So here he was, waiting for dawn, waiting for the time when he could go to her.

Because finally he'd worked things out in his fevered brain. Even if Jolie had used him, she'd done it for her father, just as she'd tried to tell him. It had finally dawned on him that he had done far worse things for his family and might very well do even worse in the future without turning a hair.

From the first, he'd seen Jolie's mystery, and he'd known there were things she wasn't telling him. He'd recognized her wariness and he'd even guessed she might have more than a passing acquaintance with fear. Initially he'd been drawn to her because of it.

In retrospect, he probably would have been able to accept anything he found out about her. With one exception. He hadn't been prepared when he had discovered that her secrets and her deceptions involved him.

He rolled over and punched his pillow. It had been a direct blow to his heart and, as a result, all reason had fled. He had made things complicated when, in the end, they were really so very simple.

He loved her and he couldn't live without her.

As soon as it was light out and he thought she'd be awake, he was going to fly to her and beg her to forgive him.

The mattress dipped as a weight came down beside him.

He jerked upright and instinctively lunged for the shape nearby.

Jolie threw out her hands, trying to grasp his arms before he could hurt her. "It's all right, Jonah. It's me."

He pushed her down to the bed, knocking

the breath out of her. Entirely fitting, she thought ruefully, since he'd been leaving her breathless since the first moment she'd seen him.

"What the hell?"

Her hands were torn away from him as he twisted and reached to turn on the bedside light.

Eyes widening, he stared down at her. "*Jolie!* My God . . ." Without another word, he pulled her upright into his arms and crushed her to him. "Jolie."

Half laughing, half crying, she held on to him. He was crushing her, but she didn't care. She'd been prepared to be greeted by a gun. She'd accept a bear hug any day. It meant he was glad to see her.

Suddenly he drew back from her so that he could see her, but he didn't release his grip on her arms. "How did you get in? The security system—"

Even in the middle of the night his intensity was emanating full force, coming at her in waves. But he wasn't frowning at her, he wasn't yelling at her. And just seeing him again made her so happy, she was having a hard time not laughing. "Right. You had a new one installed, and I must tell you, you got your money's worth. It's the best one I've ever seen."

"But you got in."

Her expression turned serious. "Yes, I did. I

got in, Jonah, without tripping a single alarm and without *using* you in any way. Just like I could have gotten through the other alarm, even if I'd never spoken a word to you. I didn't use you, Jonah. I tried, but it didn't work. I never got anything from you that could help me. Do you understand that? Do you believe me now?"

He stared at her. "You mean you broke into my house tonight to prove to me you didn't use me?"

"I couldn't figure out any other way. That's why I was praying you'd have a new system installed."

"But I was told it was invulnerable."

She smiled again. "It very nearly is. But the designer of the system didn't take into account the desperation of a woman in love."

He went motionless. "Say that again."

"I love you, Jonah. I love you with all my heart."

He slowly shook his head, dazed, amazed, incredibly happy, and intensely relieved. "I've fought a lot of battles in my life, but none of them was as hard as staying away from you these last few days. I've missed you like hell, and as soon as the sun came up, I planned to fly to you."

"Really?"

"Really."

She touched the dark shadows beneath his eyes. "You look terrible."

"You look wonderful."

"You know," she said slowly, "if this hadn't worked and I hadn't been able to convince you, I wouldn't have given up. I planned to fight for you."

"Amazing," he murmured. "I would have died fighting to win your love."

"There's no need. I love you, Jonah, and I'm going to devote the rest of my life to banishing your shadows and making sure they never come back."

"The rest of your life," he murmured huskily, drawing her to him. "I like the sound of that, but I want even more."

She laughed softly. "How about for all eternity? Would that be long enough?"

"Maybe," he said, bringing his mouth down on hers. "We'll have to see."

THE EDITORS'
CORNER

Passion and adventure reign in next month's LOVESWEPTs as irresistible heroes and unforgettable heroines find love under very unusual circumstances. When fate throws them together, it's only a matter of time before each couple discovers that danger can lead to desire. So get set to ward off the winter chill with these white-hot romances.

Helen Mittermeyer casts her spell again in **DIVINITY BROWN,** LOVESWEPT #782. They call him the black sheep of the county, a sexy ne'er-do-well who'd followed his own path—and found more than a little trouble. But when Jake Blessing comes asking for help from Divinity Brown, the curvy siren of a lawyer just can't say no! Helen Mittermeyer fashions an enthralling love story that transcends time.

Karen Leabo has long been popular with romance

readers for her fantastic love stories. So we're very pleased to present her Loveswept debut, **HELL ON WHEELS,** LOVESWEPT #783. A brash thrill-seeker who likes living on the edge isn't Victoria Holt's idea of the perfect partner for her annual tornado chase—but Roan Cullen is ready, willing, and hers! Roan revels in teasing the flame-haired meteorologist in the close quarters of the weather van, wondering if his fiery kisses can take this proper spitfire by storm. Will the forecast read: struck by lightning or love? Karen Leabo combines playful humor with sizzling sensuality in this fast-paced tale that you won't be able to put down.

Tensions run hot and steamy in Laura Taylor's **DANGEROUS SURRENDER,** LOVESWEPT #784. He'd thrown his body over hers as soon as gunfire erupted in the bank, but Carrie Forbes was shocked to feel passion mixed with fear when Brian York pulled her beneath him! The rugged entrepreneur tempts her as no man ever has, makes her crave what she thought she'd never know, but can she trust the sweet vows of intimacy when heartbreak still lingers in the shadow of her soul? Weaving a web of danger with the aphrodisiac of love on the run, Laura Taylor brilliantly explores the tantalizing threads that bind two strangers together.

Loveswept welcomes the talented Cynthia Powell, whose very first novel, **UNTAMED,** LOVESWEPT #785, rounds out this month's lineup in a very big way. "Don't move," a fierce voice commands—and Faline Eastbrook gasps at the bronzed warrior whose amber eyes sear her flesh! Brand Weston's gaze is bold, thrilling, and utterly uncivilized, but she can't let the "Wildman" see her tremble—not if she wants to capture his magnificent cats on film. Brand knows that staking his claim is reckless, but Faline has to be his. Cynthia Powell is the perfect writer for you if you love romance that's steamy, seductive, and more than a bit savage. Her sultry writing does no less than set the pages on fire!

Happy reading!

With warmest wishes,

Beth de Guzman   Shauna Summers

Senior Editor   Editor

P.S. Watch for these Bantam women's fiction titles coming in April: **MYSTIQUE**, Amanda Quick's latest bestseller, will be available in paperback. In nationally bestselling romances from RAINBOW to DEFIANT, Patricia Potter created stories that burn with the hot and dark emotions that bind a man and woman forever; now with **DIABLO**, this award-winning, highly acclaimed author sweeps readers once more into a breathtaking journey that transforms strangers into soulmates. Finally, from Geralyn Dawson comes **THE BAD LUCK WEDDING DRESS**. When her clients claim that wearing this dress is just asking for trouble, Jenny Fortune bets she can turn her luck around by wearing it at her own wedding. But first, she must find herself a groom! Be sure to see next month's LOVESWEPTs for a preview of these exceptional novels. And immediately following this page, preview the Bantam women's fiction titles on sale *now!*

Don't miss these extraordinary books
by your favorite Bantam authors

On sale in February:

GUILTY AS SIN
by Tami Hoag

BREATH OF MAGIC
by Teresa Medeiros

IVY SECRETS
by Jean Stone

Who can you trust?

Tami Hoag's impressive debut hardcover, NIGHT SINS, revealed her to be a masterful spinner of spine-chilling thrills. Now she once more tells a tale of dark suspense in . . .

GUILTY AS SIN

The kidnapping of eight-year-old Josh Kirkwood irrevocably altered the small town of Deer Lake, Minnesota. Even after the arrest of a suspect, fear maintains its grip and questions of innocence and guilt linger. Now, as Prosecutor Ellen North prepares to try her toughest case yet, she faces not only a sensation-driven press corps, political maneuvering, and her ex-lover as attorney for the defense, but an unwanted partner: Jay Butler Brooks, bestselling true-crime author and media darling, has been granted total access to the case—and to her. All the while, someone is following Ellen with deadly intent. When a second child is kidnapped while her prime suspect sits in jail, Ellen realizes that the game isn't over, it has just begun again. . . .

"If I were after you for nefarious purposes," he said as he advanced on Ellen, "would I be so careless as to approach you here?"

He pulled a gloved hand from his pocket and gestured gracefully to the parking lot, like a magician drawing attention to his stage.

"If I wanted to harm you," he said, stepping closer, "I would be smart enough to follow you home, find a way to slip into your house or garage, catch you where there would be little chance of witnesses or interference." He let those images take firm root in her mind. "That's what I would do if I were the sort of rascal who preys on women." He smiled again. "Which I am not."

"Who *are* you and what *do* you want?" Ellen demanded, unnerved by the fact that a part of her brain catalogued his manner as charming. No, not charming. Seductive. Disturbing.

"Jay Butler Brooks. I'm a writer—true crime. I can show you my driver's license if you'd like," he offered, but made no move to reach for it, only took another step toward her, never letting her get enough distance between them to diffuse the electric quality of the tension.

"I'd like for you to back off," Ellen said. She started to hold up a hand, a gesture meant to stop him in his tracks—or a foolish invitation for him to grab hold of her arm. Pulling the gesture back, she hefted her briefcase in her right hand, weighing its potential as a weapon or a shield. "If you think I'm getting close enough to you to look at a DMV photo, you must be out of your mind."

"Well, I have been so accused once or twice, but it never did stick. Now my Uncle Hooter, he's a different story. I could tell you some tales about him. Over dinner, perhaps?"

"Perhaps not."

He gave her a crestfallen look that was ruined by the sense that he was more amused than affronted. "After I waited for you out here in the cold?"

"After you stalked me and skulked around in the shadows?" she corrected him, moving another step backward. "After you've done your best to frighten me?"

"I frighten you, Ms. North? You don't strike me

as the sort of woman who would be easily frightened. That's certainly not the impression you gave at the press conference."

"I thought you said you aren't a reporter."

"No one at the courthouse ever asked," he confessed. "They assumed the same way you assumed. Forgive my pointing it out at this particular moment, but assumptions can be very dangerous things. Your boss needs to have a word with someone about security. This is a highly volatile case you've got here. Anything might happen. The possibilities are virtually endless. I'd be happy to discuss them with you. Over drinks," he suggested. "You look like you could do with one."

"If you want to see me, call my office."

"Oh, I want to see you, Ms. North," he murmured, his voice an almost tangible caress. "I'm not big on appointments, though. Preparation time eliminates spontaneity."

"That's the whole point."

"I prefer to catch people . . . off balance," he admitted. "They reveal more of their true selves."

"I have no intention of revealing anything to you." She stopped her retreat as a group of people emerged from the main doors of City Center. "I should have you arrested."

He arched a brow. "On what charge, Ms. North? Attempting to hold a conversation? Surely y'all are not so inhospitable as your weather here in Minnesota, are you?"

She gave him no answer. The voices of the people who had come out of the building rose and fell, only the odd word breaking clear as they made their way down the sidewalk. She turned and fell into step with the others as they passed.

Jay watched her walk away, head up, chin out, once again projecting an image of cool control. She didn't like being caught off guard. He would have bet money she was a list maker, a rule follower, the kind of woman who dotted all her *i*'s and crossed all her *t*'s, then double-checked them for good measure. She liked boundaries. She liked control. She had no intention of revealing anything to him.

"But you already have, Ms. Ellen North," he said, hunching up his shoulders as the wind bit a little harder and spat a sweep of fine white snow across the parking lot. "You already have."

From beloved national bestseller

Teresa Medeiros

comes an enchanting new time-travel romance

BREATH OF MAGIC

"Medeiros pens the ultimate romantic fantasy."
—Publishers Weekly

Arian Whitewood hadn't quite gotten the hang of the powerful amulet she'd inherited from her mother, but she never expected it to whisk her more than 300 years into the future. Flying unsteadily on her broomstick, she suddenly finds herself tumbling from the sky to land at the feet of Tristan Lennox. The reclusive Manhattan billionaire doesn't believe in magic, but he has his own reasons for offering one million dollars to anyone who can prove it exists.

Present-Day Manhattan

The media hadn't dubbed the four-thousand-square-foot penthouse perched at the apex of Lennox Tower "The Fortress" for nothing, Michael Copperfield thought as he changed elevators for the third time, keyed his security code into the lighted pad, and jabbed the button for the ninety-fifth floor.

The elevator doors slid open with a sibilant hiss. Resisting the temptation to gawk at the dazzling night view of the Manhattan skyline, Copperfield strode across a meadow of neutral beige carpet and shoved open the door at the far end of the suite.

"Do come in," said a dry voice. "Don't bother to knock."

Copperfield slapped that morning's edition of *The Times* on the chrome desk and stabbed a finger at the headline. "I just got back from Chicago. What in the hell is the meaning of this?"

A pair of frosty gray eyes flicked from the blinking cursor on the computer screen to the crumpled newspaper. "I should think it requires no explanation. You can't have been my PR advisor for all these years without learning how to read."

Copperfield glared at the man he had called friend for twenty-five years and employer for seven. "Oh, I can read quite well. Even between the lines." To prove his point, he snatched up the paper and read, " 'Tristan Lennox—founder, CEO, and primary stockholder of Lennox Enterprises—offers one million dollars to anyone who can prove that magic exists outside the boundaries of science. Public exhibition to be held tomorrow morning in the courtyard of Lennox Tower. Eccentric boy billionaire seeks only serious applicants.' " Copperfield twisted the paper as if to throttle his employer with it. "*Serious* applicants? Why, you'll have every psychic-hotline operator, swindler, and *Geraldo* reject on your doorstep by dawn!"

"Geraldo already called. I gave him your home number."

"How can you be so glib when I've faxed my fingers to the bone trying to establish a respectable reputation for you?"

Droll amusement glittered in Tristan's hooded eyes. "I'll give you a ten-thousand-dollar bonus if you can get them to stop calling me the 'boy billionaire.' It makes me feel like Bruce Wayne without the

Batmobile. And I did just turn thirty-two. I hardly qualify as a 'boy' anything."

"How long are you going to keep indulging these ridiculous whims of yours? Until you've completely destroyed your credibility? Until everyone in New York is laughing behind your back?"

"Until I find what I'm looking for."

"What? Or who?"

Ignoring Copperfield's pointed question, as he had for the past ten years, Tristan flipped off fax and computer with a single switch and rose from the swivel chair.

As he approached the north wall, an invisible seam widened to reveal a walk-in closet twice the size of Copperfield's loft apartment.

As Tristan activated an automated tie rack, Copperfield said, "Sometimes I think you flaunt convention deliberately. To keep everyone at arm's length where they can't hurt you." He drew in a steadying breath. "To keep the old scandal alive."

For a tense moment, the only sound was the mechanical swish of the ties circling their narrow track.

Then Tristan's shoulders lifted in a dispassionate shrug as he chose a burgundy striped silk to match his Armani suit. "Discrediting charlatans is a hobby. No different from playing the stock market or collecting Picassos." He knotted the tie with expert efficiency, shooting Copperfield a mocking glance. "Or romancing bulimic supermodels with Godiva chocolates."

Copperfield folded his arms over his chest. "Have you had my apartment under surveillance again, or did you conjure up that sordid image in your crystal ball? At least I give chocolates. As I recall, the last model I introduced you to didn't get so much as a 'thank you, ma'am' after her 'wham-bam.' "

Tristan's expression flickered with something that might have been shame in a less guarded man. "I meant to have my secretary send some flowers." He chose a pair of platinum cuff links from a mahogany tray. "If it's the million dollars you're worried about, Cop, don't waste your energy. I'm the last man who expects to forfeit that prize."

"Well, you know what they say. Within the chest of every cynic beats the heart of a disillusioned optimist."

Tristan brushed past him, fixing both his cuff links and his mask of aloof indifference firmly in place. "You should know better than anyone that I stopped believing in magic a long time ago."

"So you say, my friend," Copperfield murmured to himself. "So you say."

He pivoted only to discover that Tristan's exit had prompted the closet doors to glide soundlessly shut.

Copperfield rushed forward and began to bang on the seamless expanse with both fists. "Hey! Somebody let me out of here! Damn you, Tristan! You arrogant son of a—" A disbelieving bark of laughter escaped him as he braced his shoulder against the door. "Well, I'll be damned. What else can go wrong today?"

He found out an instant later when the mellow lighting programmed to respond solely to the mean average of his employer's heart rate flickered, then went out.

17th-Century Massachusetts

The girl plopped down on the broomstick. Her skirts bunched around her knees, baring a pair of slender calves shrouded in black stockings. A stray gust of wind rattled the dying leaves and ruffled her hair, forcing her to swipe a dark curl from her eyes. Gooseflesh prickled along her arms.

Shaking off the foreboding pall of the sky, she gripped the broomstick with both hands and screwed her eyes shut. As she attempted the freshly memorized words, a cramp shot down her thigh, shattering her concentration. She tried shouting the spell, but the broomstick did not deign to grant even a bored shudder in response.

Her voice faded to a defeated whisper. Disappointment swelled in her throat, constricting the tender membranes until tears stung her eyes. Perhaps she'd been deluding herself. Perhaps she was just as wretched a witch as she'd always feared.

She loosened the taut laces of her homespun bodice to toy with the emerald amulet suspended from a delicate filigree chain. Although she kept it well hidden from prying eyes and ignored its presence except in moments of dire vexation, she still felt compelled to wear it over her heart like a badge of shame.

"*Sacrébleu*, I only wanted to fly," she muttered.

The broomstick lurched forward, then jerked to a halt. The amulet lay cool and indifferent over her galloping heart.

Afraid to heed her own fickle senses, she slowly drew the gold chain over her head and squeezed the amulet. Leaning over the weather-beaten stick, she whispered, "I only wanted to fly."

Nothing.

She straightened, shaking her head at her own folly.

The willow broom sailed into the air and stopped, leaving her dangling by one leg. The stick quivered beneath her, the intensity of its power making the tiny hairs at her nape bristle with excitement.

"Fly!" she commanded with feeling.

The broom hung poised in midair for a shuddering eternity, then aimed itself toward the crowns of the towering oaks. It darted to a dizzying height, then swooped down, dragging her backside along the ground for several feet before shooting into another wild ascent.

She whooped in delight, refusing to consider the perils of soaring around a small clearing on a splintery hearth broom. The harder she laughed, the faster the broom traveled, until she feared it would surely bolt the clearing and shoot for the late-afternoon sky.

With a tremendous effort, she heaved herself astride the broom. She perched in relative comfort for a full heartbeat before the curious conveyance rocketed upward on a path parallel with the tallest oak, then dove downward with equal haste. The ground reached up to slam into her startled face.

She wheezed like a beached cod, praying the air would show mercy and fill her straining lungs. When she could finally breathe again, she lifted her throbbing head to find the broom lying a few feet away.

She spat out a mouthful of crumbled leaves and glared at the lifeless stick.

But her disgust was forgotten as she became aware of the gentle warmth suffusing her palm. She unfolded her trembling fingers to find the amulet bathed in a lambent glow. Her mouth fell open in wonder as the emerald winked twice as if to confirm their secret, then faded to darkness.

From the highly acclaimed author
of *First Loves* and *Sins of Innocence*

IVY SECRETS
by
Jean Stone

"Jean Stone understands the human heart."
—Literary Times

With a poignant and evocative touch, Jean Stone tells the enthralling story of three women from vastly different backgrounds bound together by an inescapable lie. They were roommates at one of New England's most prestigious colleges; now Charlie, Tess, and Marina are haunted by the truth of the past, and the fate of a young girl depends on their willingness to tell . . . Ivy Secrets.

She climbed the stairs to the fourth floor and slowly went to her room. Inside, she sat on the edge of her bed and let the tears flow quietly, the way a princess had been taught. She hated the feeling that would not go away, the feeling that there was another person inside of her, wanting to spring out, wanting to be part of the world. The world where people could talk about their feelings, could share their hopes, their dreams, their destinies not preordained. She hated that her emotions were tangled with complications, squeezed between oppressive layers of obligation, of duty. Above it all, Marina longed for Viktor; she ached for love. She held her stomach and bent forward, trying to push the torment away, willing her tears to stop.

"Marina, what's wrong?"

Marina looked up. It was Charlie. And Tess.

"Nothing." She stood, wiped her tears. "I have a dreadful headache. And cramps." There was no way these two girls—blue-collar Charlie and odd, artsy Tess—would ever understand her life, her pain.

Tess walked into the room and sat at Marina's desk. "I hate cramps," she said. "My mother calls it the curse."

"I have a heating pad, Marina," Charlie said.

"Do you want some Midol?" Tess asked.

Marina slouched back on the bed. She could no longer hold back her tears. "It is not my period," she said. "It is Viktor."

Her friends were silent.

Marina put her face in her hands and wept. It hurt, it ached, it throbbed inside her heart. She had never—ever—cried in front of anyone. But as she tried to get control of herself, the sobs grew more intense. She struggled to stop crying. She could not.

Then she felt a hand on her shoulder. A gentle hand. "Marina?" Charlie asked. "What happened?"

Marina could not take her hands from her face.

"God, Marina," Tess said, "what did he do?"

She shook her head. "Nothing," she sobbed. "Absolutely nothing."

The girls were silent again.

"It's okay," Charlie said finally. "Whatever it is, it's okay. You can tell us."

"You'll feel better," Tess added. "Honest, you will."

Slowly, Marina's sobs eased. She sniffed for a moment, then set her hands on her lap. Through her watery eyes, she saw that Charlie sat beside her; Tess had moved her chair a little closer.

"He does not understand," she said. "He does not understand how much I love him." She stood and went to the window, not wanting to see their reactions. She yanked down the window shade. "There. I said it. I love Viktor Coe. I am in love with my damn bodyguard who doesn't give a rat's ass about me."

Charlie cleared her throat.

"Jesus," Tess said.

"I love him," Marina said. "And it is impossible. He is a bodyguard. I am a princess. Neither of you have any idea how that feels. You can fall in love with any boy you meet. It does not matter. The future of a country does not matter." She flopped back on the bed. Her limbs ached, her eyes ached, her heart felt as though it had been shattered into thousands of pieces.

"Does he know you love him?" Tess asked. "Have you told him?"

"There is no point. It would only cause more problems. Besides," she added as she hung her head. "He has someone else now. I have waited too long."

"He has someone else?" Charlie asked. "Here?"

"Yes," Marina said and cast a sharp glance at Tess. "Your friend, Tess. That woman. Dell Brooks."

Tess blinked. "Dell? God, she's my mother's age."

"Viktor is not much younger. He is in his thirties."

Tess blew out a puff of air. "Are you sure, Marina? I can't believe that Dell . . ."

"Believe it. I saw it with my own two eyes."

"Maybe they're just friends," Charlie said.

Marina laughed. "Americans are so naive."

"I think you should tell him," Tess said.

"I cannot."

"Yes, you can. The problem is, you won't."

Marina studied Tess. What could this teenage misfit possibly know? Or Charlie—the goody two-shoes who thought angora sweaters were the key to happiness?

"You won't tell him because you're afraid," Tess continued. "You're afraid he doesn't feel the same way about you, and then you'll be hurt."

"You sound like you know what you're talking about," Charlie said.

Tess shrugged. "It only makes sense. We may be naive Americans, but we know that hurt's part of life. Maybe Novokia-ites—or whatever you call yourselves —don't realize that."

Marina laughed. "I believe we are called Novoki-ans."

"Novokian, schmovokian. I think you should tell the man. Get it over with."

"You might be surprised at his reaction," Charlie agreed.

Marina looked at her closed shade. Viktor thought she was tucked in for the night, he thought she was safe. He had no idea that he was the one inflicting her pain, not the strangers that he anticipated were lurking behind every bush.

She turned to Charlie and Tess—her friends. This was, she reminded herself, part of why she had come to America. She had wanted friends. She had wanted to feel like a normal girl. Maybe Charlie and Tess were more "normal" than she'd thought. And maybe, just maybe, they were right.

"Will you help me?" Marina asked. "Will you help me figure out a plan?"

On sale in March:
MYSTIQUE
by Amanda Quick

DIABLO
by Patricia Potter

THE BAD LUCK WEDDING DRESS
by Geralyn Dawson

To enter the sweepstakes outlined below, you must respond by the date specified and follow all entry instructions published elsewhere in this offer.

DREAM COME TRUE SWEEPSTAKES

Sweepstakes begins 9/1/94, ends 1/15/96. To qualify for the Early Bird Prize, entry must be received by the date specified elsewhere in this offer. Winners will be selected in random drawings on 2/29/96 by an independent judging organization whose decisions are final. Early Bird winner will be selected in a separate drawing from among all qualifying entries.

Odds of winning determined by total number of entries received. Distribution not to exceed 300 million.

Estimated maximum retail value of prizes: Grand (1) $25,000 (cash alternative $20,000); First (1) $2,000; Second (1) $750; Third (50) $75; Fourth (1,000) $50; Early Bird (1) $5,000. Total prize value: $86,500.

Automobile and travel trailer must be picked up at a local dealer; all other merchandise prizes will be shipped to winners. Awarding of any prize to a minor will require written permission of parent/guardian. If a trip prize is won by a minor, s/he must be accompanied by parent/legal guardian. Trip prizes subject to availability and must be completed within 12 months of date awarded. Blackout dates may apply. Early Bird trip is on a space available basis and does not include port charges, gratuities, optional shore excursions and onboard personal purchases. Prizes are not transferable or redeemable for cash except as specified. No substitution for prizes except as necessary due to unavailability. Travel trailer and/or automobile license and registration fees are winners' responsibility as are any other incidental expenses not specified herein.

Early Bird Prize may not be offered in some presentations of this sweepstakes. Grand through third prize winners will have the option of selecting any prize offered at level won. All prizes will be awarded. Drawing will be held at 204 Center Square Road, Bridgeport, NJ 08014. Winners need not be present. For winners list (available in June, 1996), send a self-addressed, stamped envelope by 1/15/96 to: Dream Come True Winners, P.O. Box 572, Gibbstown, NJ 08027.

THE FOLLOWING APPLIES TO THE SWEEPSTAKES ABOVE:

No purchase necessary. No photocopied or mechanically reproduced entries will be accepted. Not responsible for lost, late, misdirected, damaged, incomplete, illegible, or postage-die mail. Entries become the property of sponsors and will not be returned.

Winner(s) will be notified by mail. Winner(s) may be required to sign and return an affidavit of eligibility/release within 14 days of date on notification or an alternate may be selected. Except where prohibited by law, entry constitutes permission to use of winners' names, hometowns, and likenesses for publicity without additional compensation. Void where prohibited or restricted. All federal, state, provincial, and local laws and regulations apply.

All prize values are in U.S. currency. Presentation of prizes may vary; values at a given prize level will be approximately the same. All taxes are winners' responsibility.

Canadian residents, in order to win, must first correctly answer a time-limited skill testing question administered by mail. Any litigation regarding the conduct and awarding of a prize in this publicity contest by a resident of the province of Quebec may be submitted to the Regie des loteries et courses du Quebec.

Sweepstakes is open to legal residents of the U.S., Canada, and Europe (in those areas where made available) who have received this offer.

Sweepstakes in sponsored by Ventura Associates, 1211 Avenue of the Americas, New York, NY 10036 and presented by independent businesses. Employees of these, their advertising agencies and promotional companies involved in this promotion, and their immediate families, agents, successors, and assignees shall be ineligible to participate in the promotion and shall not be eligible for any prizes covered herein. SWP 3/95

DON'T MISS THESE FABULOUS
BANTAM WOMEN'S FICTION TITLES